SUPERB WRITING
TO FIRE THE IMAGINATION

Maggie Pearson writes: 'More than half the time, I'm living in an imaginary world. If you took all the books out of my house, it would probably fall down! When I'm not reading other people's stories, I'm making up my own. I'm sort of a cross between a magpie and a vampire; everything I see and hear gets filed away inside my head, where the ideas shift around until a pattern begins to form and another story surfaces. Sometimes I get the spooky feeling that the stories exist already in some parallel world, before I've written a word.

My dad was a brilliant story-teller. He used to escape from the boring work he did all day via his imagination, making up weird and wonderful bedtime stories for my sister and me, and ending with a cliff-hanger every night. It's from him that I get my love of fast-moving plots, quirky characters and standing ideas on their head to see if they look more interesting that way up.

We'd all like to live in a perfect world, wouldn't we? Or would we? Happy families, sunshine all day long, food at the press of a button, no crime, no pollution . . . Bo-ring! The really hard bit was trying to imagine the world outside the Omega Seven Colony, with life-forms unlike anything that ever evolved on Earth. Maybe you can do better?'

Also by Maggie Pearson:

Owl Light
A W H Smith Mind Boggling Book
Night People
Alien Dawn
Dark of the Moon

Other titles available from Hodder Silver:

Law of the Wolf Tower
Wolf Star Rise
Tanith Lee

The Brugan
Stephen Moore

Silverwing
Sunwing
Kenneth Opel

Mirror Mirror
Louise Cooper

OMEGA SEVEN

MAGGIE PEARSON

Hodder Children's Books

a division of Hodder Headline

First published in Great Britain in 1999
by Hodder Children's Books
as part of Hodder Silver Series

10 9 8 7 6 5 4 3 2

A Catalogue record for this book is available from
the British Library

ISBN 0 340 73658 5

Typeset by Avon Dataset Ltd, Bidford-on-Avon, Warks

Printed and bound in Great Britain by
The Guernsey Press Co. Ltd, Channel Isles

Hodder Children's Books
A Division of Hodder Headline
338 Euston Road
London NW1 3BH

In Italy for thirty years under the Borgias they had warfare, terror, murder, bloodshed – they produced Michaelangelo, Leonardo da Vinci and the Renaissance.

In Switzerland, they had brotherly love, five hundred years of democracy and peace and what did they produce? The cuckoo clock.

Orson Welles

Whilst part of what we perceive comes through our senses from the object before us, another part (and it may be the larger part) always comes out of our own mind.

William James

ONE

Knock, knock!
Who's there?
Luke.
Luke who?
Look out of the window and you'll see.

Luke, that's me. I'll be your guide to Omega Seven, the best of all possible worlds. No pollution. No crime. No worries. No cares. Peace and love and sunshine all the way.

Welcome to Paradise!

I got my first inkling that all was not hunky-dory on this best of all possible worlds when the autocook served up curry for breakfast the third morning in a row.

Stuff like that is not supposed to happen on the Paradise Planet. Things Do Not Go Wrong.

As I came out of my room and started down the stairs to the living area, I heard Ma's voice, 'I don't believe it! It's curry again! At least, it *looks* like curry.' She sniffed at it gingerly: 'It *smells* like curry.'

'Curry – and rice?' suggested Pa – not very hopefully – punching a couple more buttons on the autocook. Another plate of food appeared.

'No rice,' I said, from my vantage-point on the stairway. 'Just curry.'

They both turned and looked at me as if it was somehow my fault. I shrugged. Not me, not this time.

Pa was already halfway to making a swift exit. 'I'll grab a bite to eat when I get to work,' he said. 'Call Maintenance this time. Get them to fix it.' You'd expect a telepath to know better. Then, digging himself into an even deeper hole, he added, 'Why didn't you call them yesterday?'

'Why don't *you* call them?' Ma snapped. But her heart wasn't in it.

'Got to go,' he said as he slipped out the door. 'Lee and Fitz are both on-line, and there's a message about to come in from Starbase Five. Have a nice day.'

Telepaths can do that to you. Any time Life's Highway looks like getting a bit rocky, they're suddenly needed somewhere else and there's no way you can call them a liar.

'Nice day,' I said, as the door slid gently shut behind him. You can't even slam a door on Omega Seven. The first rule of the Colony is 'Stay Calm'.

I said to Ma, 'Shouldn't you be going too?' She didn't answer. She just stood there, staring at the four plates of curry, like she was wondering whether they might make a nice hologram.

'Stay calm,' I told her. 'I'll call Maintenance.'

Under the spiral stair the communicator-unit sits, looking cheerfully expectant, like a dog waiting for someone to say 'Walkies!' The Company likes you to keep in touch.

I flashed my ID, and the comm-U twinkled into life: 'Good morning, Luke! You have – No – messages this morning. Isn't it a lovely day? Are you having a nice day? I know *I* am.'

'No,' I said. 'We're not.'

'Oh, dear! I *am* sorry to hear that!' (It didn't sound it.) 'What seems to be the trouble?'

'Curry for breakfast.'

'That's new!'

'It's the third day running.'

'That's not good. That's *bad*. I'll put you through to Welfare.'

'No!' I reached for the Strike button, but I wasn't quick enough. I was on-line to the Company Welfare Department.

If I was ship-wrecked in a shark-infested sea (which isn't very likely, I admit, since there's no water within a thousand miles that a three-year-old couldn't stand up in – but if I was) I'd sooner take my chance with the barracudas than climb aboard a raft crewed by the Welfare.

Today it was Sweet-as-sugar.

'Good morning Luke,' she cooed, and I began to get that old familiar feeling that someone was pouring treacle over me from a great height. 'How may I help you?'

'You can't,' I said.

'I can try,' she wheedled. 'Tell me about it.'

'OK. There's nothing but curry for breakfast again.'

'Hm. That's not exactly an ideal diet for a growing boy. It seems to me your parents could do with a little counselling. Do you have any other complaints?'

'No!' I yelped. 'It's not their fault.' I wasn't about to let myself be carted off to join the dormitory kids while Welfare sorted out my parents for me. The dormitory kids – DKs, or deeks for short – they're weird.

Stay Calm, right?

'It's the autocook,' I told her. 'Whatever order we punch in we just get curry.'

'That's not a problem for Welfare, Luke.'

'I know.'

'You should call Maintenance.'

'I know.'

'Then why are you wasting my time?'

'The comm-U gave me the wrong number.'

'Well, you'd better ask it for the right one, hadn't you?' she snapped. I caught a satisfying whiff of pure vitriol before she was her sugary self again. 'And remember, Luke, if there's any little problem bothering you – anything at all – we're here to help you. Have a nice day.'

I signalled 'End', but I was still connected.

After an awkward pause, her voice oozed out, 'I didn't hear you, Luke.'

'Nice day,' I mumbled.

The comm-U went dead. I ran my ID past it again.

'Good morning, Luke! It *is* nice to be talking to you again so soon! Are you having a nice day? I know *I*—'

'Forget it,' I said, hitting the Off button. I'll walk round.' I had no classes that day. I could call in at Maintenance on my way to the Leisure Drome.

In the living-area the table was clear, and the waste disposal was chugging away contentedly in the background. It was getting quite a taste for curry. Ma stood with her arms folded, watching it. Suddenly she spoke.

'Once upon a time, on Earth, I had a nice, old-fashioned, *reliable* microwave. You always knew what you were going to get out because you knew what you'd just put in. What could be simpler?'

I felt I ought to put in a word for Progress.

'The autocook's supposed to be simpler. No shopping. No time wasted. No mess. Just press a few buttons and – hey presto! – a perfectly balanced meal in the flavour and texture of your choice. Or not.' I caught the look on Ma's face. 'I'll go round to Maintenance now. Get them to see to it while you're at work.'

I'm not prejudiced myself, but a lot of people prefer to have the 'droids in to fix things while they're not around. Looks like a man; acts like a machine. That's spooky.

'Let the Company take care of it,' I added encouragingly. She muttered something under her breath. It sounded like 'Sod the Company!'

But I couldn't be sure.

'Have a nice day,' I said.

'Nice day,' she answered glumly, as I went out.

TWO

Outside, the weather was perfect, as usual. Bright blue sky, with exactly the right number of fluffy white clouds strung out across it. Just enough breeze to keep the air fresh. Temperature in the mid-to-high twenties.

Of course, the Company doesn't organise the weather on Omega Seven. Even the Company can't do that – yet. But the naturally perfect weather was what made them finally plump for Omega Seven as the site for their experimental colony. The way they saw it, everywhere on Earth these days, Life has a habit of getting in the way of Progress. Grade-A scientific brains waste valuable thinking-time wondering what the kids are getting up to in school and what to cook for dinner and whether this is the day they finally get mugged and will it rain, even though the forecast said fine. That's before they move on to global cooling and water rationing and the last great deserts being turned into theme-parks. You can worry about it all, but you can't change it.

So the Company figured if they set up a research operation somewhere far enough away, where you never even got to hear about all that stuff, that would give *their* scientists the edge over the competition. Happy families, with perfectly-run lives, equals cutting-edge research – and fat profits.

They went hunting round for their paradise planet. And they lit on Omega Seven. Perfect weather. Pleasant scenery. Nothing poisonous or dangerous to humans. No poor people. No pollution. No traffic jams. No crime.

Omega Seven: the Perfect Planet for Perfect People.

Dullsville. The boringest place in the Entire Universe.

Except for the Blue Mountain. The Blue Mountain still carried a last shred of mystery about it. A forlorn hope. Above the house-tops, between the matt white of the Admin Block and the opaque glass of the Leisure Drome, I caught a glimpse of it in the distance.

The first landing-party, catching sight of the Blue Mountain on the horizon, had sent the nearest telepaths into overdrive (and a couple into early retirement) with excited messages about a great alien city. That set a few alarm systems ringing back on Earth. After centuries of searching! Of saying how great it would be to know we're not the only intelligent life-form in the Universe. Not alone.

Now they weren't so sure.

Let's not over-react, they said. Proceed with caution. Let the natives know we're friendly, but keep all weapons on red-alert.

For nearly a month the Earth, and all the settled worlds, and every space-station in between, held their collective breath before the verdict finally came through. The 'city' was just a giant, crystal-like formation of solid rock. Smooth as glass. Scans showed it was solid, through and through. The explorers attacked it with hammers and chisels. Then with diamond drills. Blasters, lasers, plasma bolts and good, old-fashioned TNT. They also kicked it and shouted at it, which had about as much effect as everything else they'd tried. Not a dent. Not a scratch. The Blue Mountain was harder than anything known to human science. A mystery. But harmless. Apparently.

What was it made of? How did it get there? There wasn't a kid on Omega Seven who didn't believe s/he could find the answers, if only s/he could get close enough to touch those rocks.

But the Blue Mountain was off-limits; well outside the force-field that surrounded the colony, keeping us all safely fenced in. Though what they thought they were keeping us safe from, on a planet with no known dangers . . . Maybe the Company just likes to feel it's in control.

So, anyway, here's me, on this third curry-for-breakfast morning, strolling into the Maintenance Office, crossing a floor so squeaky-clean I could hear my feet leaving scuff-marks.

The place was huge, built to impress, though I tried hard not to be. Walls covered with screens and controls; shiny metal pipes snaking up and down; bubbles of coloured light rising and falling in transparent tubes; and cyber-units, like big, shiny beetles, scurrying everywhere.

OK. I was impressed.

The one human face, rugged and dependable above his sunshine-yellow, dirt-repellent work-suit, looked like an imposter among all this glittering hi-tech. His proper place was somewhere out at the cutting edge of the galaxy, nursing a stricken starcruiser safely home on a wonky warp-drive with nothing but a sonic screwdriver and a few well-chosen prayers. But his badge, when I got close enough to read it, reassured me that he was MainTech One.

'ID,' he said.

'Please?' I prompted, passing my bracelet over the scanner. He squinted up at me, head tilted a little to one side, dead-pan. A guy with attitude. My kind of person. 'What can I do for you, Luke?' he said.

I explained about the curry.

He punched a couple of buttons, then sat back again. 'Let the Company take care of it,' he said comfortably. 'I'll send a 'droid round in the morning.'

I said, 'Can't you get it done today?'

He shook his head. 'Sorry. Not today.'

'Only, I sort of promised Ma.' I was still hopeful. In the recharging bays behind him, I could see a spare 'droid idling. 'Couldn't you send him?' I pointed.

'Not today,' said MainTech One. 'Company regulations, see. All work schedules for the day shift to be completed and reported to Central Control by oh-nine-hundred hours.' He glanced at his ID bracelet which, like mine, doubled as a watch. 'It's now – oh-nine-oh-seven. You should have called in from home. *Then* you'd have been in time. *And* saved yourself a walk.'

'Thanks,' I said. 'I did. At least, I tried. The comm-U put me through to Welfare.'

'Ah!' He nodded, understanding. I sensed a kindred spirit.

'So, you see, I *would* have been in time.'

'Not my fault.'

My mistake. Forget it. Still, I decided to give it one last try. 'Is that 'droid just going to sit idling away in the corner all day?'

'That's right.'

'That's stupid.'

'Don't blame me, son. I didn't make the rules. Trust the Company. The Company knows best. Let me give you a word of warning.' He leaned his elbows on the desk and beckoned me closer, lowering his voice. 'Don't you, or any of your family, go trying to fix that autocook for yourselves before he gets there. Curry's nothing to what one family went through. I could tell you a tale . . .'

And he did.

'There was this family, see? Very much like yours, I 'spect. Pa, Ma and Junior. A girl, not a boy, but that's by the way. Came in here, they did, all three of them together. I wasn't here myself, but . . .

' "Our autocook's gone," they said.

' "Gone? You mean broken," says the duty man.

' "We mean gone. Vanished. Disappeared. Vamoosed. Gone AWOL. It is no longer there."

'That's what they told him. That's what he told me. "Gone walkabout on its little legs, had it?' I said. "Sprouted wings and flown away?" ' MainTech One glanced round at the 'droid in the corner, to see if it was enjoying the joke. It wasn't. The 'droid hasn't been programmed yet that can cotton on to a joke. He sighed. I pulled a face, to show I knew the feeling.

'Well!' he went on. 'If it was gone, that wasn't a job for Maintenance, was it? We can't maintain what's not there. Lost Property, that's a job for Security. Security sent a man round. There was the "missing" autocook, large as life, but before Security could file a report, here's the same family (Ma, Pa and the littl'un) – back again. Pa's carrying a baked potato in his hand. "Look at this!" he says. Cuts it open, here on this very desk. What do you think was inside?' I shook my head.

'A dob of jam, just like you find in a doughnut. "That's a good trick," my mate says. "Trick nothing!" says Pa. "Try eating it! Try eating it with beef stew that tastes of chocolate. Try your morning porridge flavoured with fish!" '

He paused to see what effect this was having on me. I mimed suitable astonishment. Puzzlement. Pray-continue. Whatever.

'This was no job for a 'droid,' he said.

I nodded sagely.

'My mate called me in to hold the fort while he went round himself to look at this autocook of theirs.'

'And?'

'*And* he could see what the trouble was right away.' He leaned forward: 'They'd been *fiddling*!'

'Fiddling?' I said.

He nodded: 'Fiddling. It was like they'd taken the innards out of that autocook, shuffled them about a bit, then shoved them back again, all anyhow. They denied it, of course. All knowledge. "It wasn't us," they said. "Whoever took it – he's the one." "Like who?" we said. Everyone's got an autocook. Who'd want two? Trying to cover up what they'd done, o'course. Fiddling with Company property, that's a serious offence.' He shook his head sadly. 'Even when they were being loaded on to the hopper home, they still kept insisting it wasn't them. Anyway,' he finished triumphantly, '*that*'s what comes of fiddling, see? So hands off! OK?'

'OK,' I said.

'Tomorrow morning, without fail, I'll send a 'droid round. I'll make it this one, if you like. He's free then.'

'He's free now,' I pointed out.

'Have a nice day,' he said firmly. The door slid open about a hundred metres behind me.

I can take a hint. 'Nice day,' I said. 'Missing you already.'

It wasn't a nice day. It was coming up to nine-thirty, and the hole where my breakfast should have been felt like it was trying to eat me from inside.

THREE

I stood outside the Maintenance Office and I thought to myself, So! So it wasn't just our autocook that was acting strange. Or was it? Was MainTech One's story no more than that – a story?

I should have been checking in at the Leisure Drome by now, but, what the heck . . .

Five minutes later, I was presenting my ID at the door of the Science Complex.

'G'day, Luke,' said the door, keeping itself firmly shut. 'Whom did you wish to see?'

'Dr Pavlov, please.'

'Dr Pavel Pavlovitch Pavlov?'

'Is there another Dr Pavlov?' (There isn't.)

'I am not programmed to give that information,' the door said primly.

I said, 'It's always Dr Pavlov I come to see. Why don't you remember?'

'I am not programmed to remember. If you would remember to answer properly when I ask the question, we wouldn't have to go through this every time.'

'You *do* remember!'

'Remember what?' the door said smartly. 'I am not programmed to remember. Shall we start again? And try to get it right this time. Ready? Right! Now. *Whom* did you wish to see?'

I took a deep breath. 'Dr Pavel Pavlovitch Pavlov.

Omega Ecology Survey. In the basement,' I added helpfully.

'I *know*!' snapped the door. 'You don't have to tell me. OK, you can come in now.' I slid inside and hurried downstairs before it could remember to ask me if I'd got an appointment.

The sign on the door was scribbled in pencil on a scrap of ragged paper.

OMEGA ECOLOGY SURVEY
Dr P P Pavlov

Pavel is one of the last of your pencil-and-paper men. And he wears glasses. No Alpha wears glasses these days. Security were right on the ball; they picked out Pavel by his glasses the moment he stepped off the hopper. For a while they had the telepaths on full alert, checking out Dr P P Pavlov through all the known worlds.

But he was clean. And Alpha-Plus. Seems it wasn't the Company that had sent him. It was the official world government, the Government of Independent Terran States. Some terrocrat had spotted a bit in the small print of the Constitution, about 'seeking out new life and new civilisations', which they'd overlooked when they made over Omega Seven to the Company. The Company still didn't like it much, but there was nothing they could do once Pavel's Security clearance came through. Except have the 'droids clear out one of the basement store-rooms and leave Dr P P Pavlov to get on with his ecology survey.

He'd had to scrape together most of the equipment

he needed by begging, borrowing or intercepting odd bits and pieces on their way to being recycled, because nothing gets thrown away on Omega Seven, not after the cost of freighting it halfway across the galaxy. (*Want not, waste not*, as the Company puts it.) What he couldn't get hold of, he used to patch together himself, with more enthusiasm than DIY-manship. I managed to slide the door open just wide enough to squeeze inside.

'I called out, 'Hi, Pavel!'

'G'day, Luke. Over here!'

I took a fix on his voice and set out through the Scrapheap Jungle, careful not to brush against anything, in case I started a domino-effect. Checked out the tripede which, as near as I could judge, was standing on the identical spot where I'd seen it two days ago, three-square on its little legs, its one purple eye glaring. The food-bowl was empty, though.

From the very first moment Pavel brought it in and popped it inside this blue-glass tank he'd borrowed from somewhere or other, that tripede had made up its mind it was going to walk right out again. It kept coming up against the glass barrier – bump! – sitting down suddenly, then getting up and trying again. It got pretty angry when it found it couldn't do it.

Pavel said that was just the way its face happened to be arranged. It couldn't be angry; it didn't know how. Anger and fear (says Pavel) are responses that creatures on Earth have developed for their protection and survival. Here on Omega Seven, no-one eats anyone else and there's always plenty of food to go round. So: nothing to get angry – or frightened – about. Ever.

Maybe. That tripede still looked pretty mad to me.

Standing stock-still, sulking. I pulled a face at it as I edged past. The eye glared back, following me.

I pulled another face. 'How does it feel to be really, *really* stupid?'

Still it glared.

'If you weren't stupid, you'd have thought of another way out by now. Try piling up the rocks, so you can climb over. Or throwing them.'

Pavel peered at me round a tottering pile of debris. 'You sound like the cat that got the sour cream today,' he said. 'What's got into you?'

'Nothing,' I said, with feeling. 'Not even breakfast.'

'Ah! Help yourself – in the corner.' Pavel was always fetching food from the dispenser upstairs, then forgetting to eat it by the time he got back. No wonder he was so skinny.

I moseyed over and stretched out a hand to what looked like a carton of popcorn.

'No, not that one!' Eyes in the back of his head. 'One of the miners brought that in last night. Don't eat it before I've had a chance to analyse it. Try the carton next to it.' He hunched back down again over the geno-scanner, jotting pencil notes on the back of a piece of wrapping paper.

I picked up the container and peeled back the lid. Chocolate shake. Probably.

'So what happened to your breakfast?' he asked, without looking up. In between slurps of frothy chocolate, I explained about the curry problem. Pavel smiled to himself, still peering at the scanner. Didn't comment.

I fixed myself a peanut butter and pastrami sandwich,

imagining what Welfare would have to say about unsuitable eating habits for a growing boy, if they knew. And felt better than I had since I got up that morning. So I pushed a tray of silica-based life-forms out of the way and hitched myself up on to the work surface.

Pavel was still going through the motions, finishing the run he'd set up for himself, but I could see he was getting nowhere. Muttering. Tapping his teeth with his pencil. At last he flung the pencil down, pushed back his chair so hard it hit the cupboard behind, screwed up his notes and batted them into a corner. Somewhere between a yell and a sigh, he announced, 'This is impossible!'

'Still no sign of a food-chain?' I said, as sympathetic as I could be through a mouthful of peanut and pastrami.

He shook his head. 'Nothing! Not the smallest thread.'

Pavel says there has to be a system. On every planet where there's life, there's a system: species interlinked in order to survive. Feeding off one another. Fighting for survival. Or learning to co-operate. Except here, on Omega Seven. Here, they don't fight, or co-operate; they just do their own thing. Separate species. Each one with its own food-source. All vegetarian.

'What can you do with such a planet?' he demanded.

'Call it Paradise?' I suggested, working a bit of pastrami from between my teeth.

'And yet . . .' he added. He sat easing the stiffness out of his shoulders, eyes fixed on the screen again, frowning. 'Sometimes I get the strangest feeling that there is something very obvious I am missing.'

'Take a break. Maybe when you're not looking, the answer'll sneak up on you.' He nodded, unfolded himself from his chair and stood up.

'Have something to eat,' I suggested. 'I always find that helps.'

'Thank you. I will.' He wandered down to the end of the workbench and came back with a drink of some kind.

Partly to take his mind off his own worries, mainly because I wanted to know what he thought about it anyway, I told him the story of the vanishing autocook, just as MainTech One had told it to me. More or less. I may have added a few twiddly bits of my own, the way you do – hot ice-cream; baked beans in custard instead of tomato sauce.

Pavel put his drink down again – I don't think he'd touched it – swivelled his chair round and leaned back against the workbench, quietly polishing his glasses, looking improbably young in spite of his grey hairs. When I finished, he popped the glasses back on his nose again, peered at me solemnly and nodded. 'Uh-huh! And what do you make of this story?'

'You mean, do I think it's true? What do you think?'

He shook his head. 'No, no! I asked you first. What do *you* think?'

'I don't know.' I thought about it. It was funny, in my mind's eye now, I could almost see her. The girl . . . Brown curls and freckles. The sort of girl it might have happened to. But then, she'd have had to have been in school for a while.

Would I – could I? – have forgotten her, almost, quite so soon?

I said slowly: 'It could be true. Just about. Couldn't it? But it's not, is it?'

Pavel shrugged. 'How do I know? I wasn't there. I do know that people need such stories. They like to believe strange things might happen.' He pressed a button and the scanner finally went blank. 'Shouldn't you be in school?'

I shook my head. 'I've got no classes today. I'm supposed to be at the Leisure Drome.'

There was the faintest pause, then, 'How would you like to be my assistant for the day instead? Let's go out!'

I said, 'Out? As in O-U-T – Out? You mean – the Outlands?' Pavel was already on the move, collecting up bits of equipment. Over his shoulder, he said, 'Just as far as the Blue Mountain.'

'The Blue Mountain?' I squeaked.

'I have instruments left out there which need checking, observations to make, food to collect for that little fellow there . . .' He nodded towards the tripede, who seemed to prick up his non-existent ears at the mention of food. My imagination. Tripedes don't understand English.

'You don't have to come,' said Pavel, 'if you think you'll be bored.' *Bored*? I was so un-bored, I couldn't speak. 'But I could use some help.'

'OK,' I said. 'If you need my help. Of course I'll come.'

WOW! And I'd thought this was going to be just another day in Dullsville! I waited outside, with Pavel's gear clustering round my feet, while he fetched the hovercar. I remember glancing at the time – not ten-thirty yet – and marvelling to myself at how suddenly the day had totally changed. In a few more minutes, we were on our way, gliding through the streets almost empty of people at this time of day, stopping at the perimeter gate.

'IDs, please,' said the guard.

Pavel went first. Check. No problem. Coolly, I stuck out my wrist for the scanner, as if a trip to the Outlands was all in a day's work to me.

But there was nothing to scan. My wrist was empty. I goggled at it like an idiot; how could it be empty? I checked my pockets. Then I started scrabbling about inside the car, on the seat under me, and down the sides. With growing panic – you do not lose your ID just like that! An ID is unloseable – I carried out a fingertip search of the floor under my feet, then crawled over the rest of the car, places I'd been nowhere near.

'You've dropped it in the lab, maybe,' Pavel suggested. 'We'll go back.'

I knew there was no point in going back. I remembered glancing at the time again – unnecessarily, the way you do – as I climbed into the car and the door slid to behind me. If my ID had dropped off on the ground then, I would have seen it go. It had to be inside the car; but it wasn't.

Pavel did his best for me. 'This boy is acting as my assistant. For him it is a learning opportunity, not to be missed. I'm sure his teachers would agree, if you like to check with them.'

I tried straight grovelling: 'Can't I go anyway? Please! It's not for long. Just a couple of hours. You can check me out yourself, personally, and check me back in. No-one'll know.'

The guard was adamant: 'More than my job's worth.'

I could not believe this. 'Why is everyone so keen to

stay on this boring planet anyway?'

'A tour of duty in the mines of Cerebos might sound like fun to you,' said the guard. 'But I've tried it. Believe me, boring's better.'

'Stay calm, Luke,' said Pavel. 'I'm sorry. But I really do have to go now.'

'Instruments to check, right? Food for the tripede.'

'Another time I'll take you. The next free day you have, I promise.'

'If you want,' I said, barely moving my lips. I stood beside the guard and watched the hovercar beetling away across the plain towards the Blue Mountain. I'll tell you another odd thing about it. Sometimes it looks so close you feel you could almost reach out and touch it. Something to do with the light, it's supposed to be. But you turn away, and it's still like the mountain's peering over your shoulder. That particular day, it seemed like a million miles away.

'It'll turn up,' said the guard. 'Your ID. Things do, don't they? Did you hear about the autocook that—?'

'Yes,' I said. 'I did.'

'Well, anyway,' she said, 'look on the bright side. It could be raining.'

'No, it couldn't,' I said.

It never rains on Omega Seven, except at night.

FOUR

I strolled on down to the Leisure Drome. There didn't seem to be anywhere else to go. Ma would be at work by now. Without my ID I couldn't even get into my own home.

Standing outside the Leisure Drome, it suddenly struck me that I couldn't get in there either; not without an ID.

I never much cared for the place before, Welfare always on the watch. Sweet-as-sugar making sure you didn't go in for too much violent exercise. Tough-and-manly keeping an eye open, catch you sitting around too long and it would be hurry-hurry-hurry! on down to the gym, where they're getting up two teams for basketball, whatever. *We want you to grow up to be a well-balanced individual, Luke*. Like they were training a team of tightrope walkers. Today, knowing I couldn't get in, inside the Drome was where I really wanted to be. I stood, watching the people going in and out. Flash your ID; the door slides open. Walk inside; the door slides shut.

No visual scan, as far as I could see.

I thought I could see a way it might be done, with a bit of help. Getting in. The snag was, everyone in my group would be inside already. Then I spotted one of the dormitory kids strolling across the promenade.

Looking back, from where I am now, I'd say this was Fate, with a capital F.

He was homing in on the Leisure Drome with that

not-quite-with-you look the deeks all wear. Like I said, the deeks are weird. No families. No friends. Each one keeping to his-or-her own schedule. They don't even talk to each other much. I could have let him go – maybe I should have done – waited for someone I knew better. And everything would have turned out different. Of course, I didn't know that at the time. At the time, all I was thinking was, needs must. I was determined to get inside the Leisure Drome and this might be my only chance.

What was his name? Something short . . . Tim? No. Tom? Tam?

I slid between him and the door before he could present his ID.

What the heck was his name? Tam was close. Close, but no cigar. I ransacked my memory-banks. Ram? Rambo? Jumbo? Be serious now! You're only going to get one shot at this. Big brown eyes staring up at me didn't help.

I fast-forwarded through the alphabet and finally plumped: 'Hi, Sam!' Casual but friendly.

'G'day.' Big brown eyes still staring, giving nothing away.

'It is Sam, isn't it?'

'Yes—?'

'Luke,' I said. My jaw was beginning to set rigid in what had started out as a warm smile.

He put me in mind of some of the specimens in Pavel's laboratory. Not worried, or angry; just waiting for me to move out of the way, so he could get on with his life. Don't let the glazed look fool you; the deeks are off-the-chart-smart, every one.

I said, 'Did you hear about the dumb 'droid who sat up all night, wondering where the sun had got to?'

Sam shook his head.

'In the morning it dawned on him.'

He smiled – almost. Loosened up a little anyway.

'Sam,' I said. 'I've got a problem – er – a theory I want to try out. Would you like to help me with a little experiment?'

'–?–'

I held up my wrist and jiggled it about: 'Look! No ID. I want to see how far I can get without it. First thing is to find out if it's possible to get inside the Leisure Drome.'

'–?–' At least he was still interested.

There wasn't much to explain. As far as I could make out, once an ID had been presented the scanner only checked bodies, not numbers of arms and legs. If two people went through together, arm-in-arm, keeping in step, there was no way it would know the difference.

'OK,' said Sam. It was pretty small potatoes, I suppose, to your average genius.

So that's what we did. We stood, arms round each others' shoulders like the best of buddies. He flashed his ID at the scanner, and – by the left! – we marched in.

I don't know about Sam; I was holding my breath. But . . . no-one stopped us. No alarm bells rang. No Security units sprang out of hiding. No stun-guns. Too easy.

'What are you going to do now?' Sam asked.

Good question. Once inside, the joys of the Leisure Drome are yours for the asking. All you have to do is present your ID. Houston, we have a problem. No ID.

'Come and play chess, why don't you?' suggested Sam.

'I often check out a board to play against myself.'

It's the sort of thing the deeks are allowed to do. It wasn't hard to see why. After he'd beaten me three times in twelve minutes flat, I said: 'Sorry, Sam. You'd better find someone else.'

Sam said placidly, 'Don't apologise. I like the way you play. I don't know from one move to the next whether you're being really smart or amazingly stupid.'

'Thanks,' I said, getting up to leave. 'Have fun.'

'Sorry,' he said at once. 'I didn't mean . . . I'm not very good with people. I'm brilliant at numbers, though.' His little round face brightened: 'Test me! Give me a date!'

'A date?'

'Any date! Day, month and year.'

'What for?'

'Just do it.'

I sat down again. 'OK. June . . . 24th! 19 – um – 76.'

There came a second's pause; no more. 'It was a Thursday,' he said.

'Was it?' Was I supposed to applaud or something?

'Don't you know?'

'Of course I don't!'

'Then what did you ask me for?'

'It was your idea!'

'Sorry. That used to be a kind of a party-piece. Sorry,' he said again.

'It's OK.'

'If you'd rather talk algorithms or prime number theory . . .'

'No, no, no!' I held up my hands in surrender. Party pieces were about my weight. 'All right, Mr Mathematical Genius, here's one for you: ready?'

He nodded.

I recited, very fast: 'As I was going to St Ives,

I met a man with seven wives.

Every wife had seven sacks.

In every sack were seven cats.

Every cat had seven kits.

Kits, cats, sacks and wives;

How many were going to St Ives?'

This time he didn't even blink. 'Two thousand seven hundred and fifty three,' he said.

'Wrong!' I yelled.

'You're not counting the sacks as people? In that case, it would be—'

'You're still wrong. Wrong, wrong, wrong! The answer's one, you drone! If *I* met *them* and *I'm* going *to* St Ives, all the rest must be coming away.'

He chewed his lip. Then he said sulkily, 'There could be a side-road, feeding in to the main one going there. Or something.'

'Well there isn't. Wasn't. Right?' Perhaps I was being a bit hard on him; the deeks don't mix much with normal people. I said, 'Is it a trick or something? That stuff with dates? Is it something I could learn?'

He shook his head: 'I can't explain it. It's just something I can do.'

'Wish I was better at maths.'

'What's your speciality?'

Tricky one. 'I haven't been assigned yet.' Mr Strangeways, the Studies Supervisor, said that with Ma and Pa both Alphas – and Pa a telepath, too – I was bound to turn out to be good at something. Eventually. But lately I'd been catching a note of desperation in his voice. I tried not to let it get me down. Pavel said some people were just late developers.

'I think I might be an ecologist,' I said.

'Like Dr Pavlov?'

'I s'pose.' Pavel was none of his business.

Sam picked up the bad vibes. He changed the subject: 'You want to go swimming?'

I pointed out that I'd got no ID: no ID, no bathers.

'It'll be all right,' said Sam, suddenly taking charge. 'Come on!' So I followed him down to the pool.

I'm shorter than you,' he said. 'But we're about the same size round.' He flashed his ID at the dispenser which coughed up a pair of bathing trunks.

'Hope you like purple,' he said. 'It's my favourite colour.'

'For me? What are you going to wear?'

'I'll just watch you. Go on.' He thrust them into my hands and wandered off towards the spectators' area. So I changed into the purple bathers, dry-showered and went through to the pool. Caught Sam's eye, sitting there. He waved and smiled. Weird, I thought; seriously weird.

I dived in and swam up and down for a bit. Rode the flumes once or twice. Dived off the boards several times, including one perfect back-flip, which should have pleased me no end. But whenever I looked around, there was Sam, watching. After a while I climbed out and went over and asked him again: 'Are you sure you don't want to swim? We can swap.'

He shook his head. 'I don't swim.'

'Everybody swims.'

'I don't.' He sat, arms hugging his bony knees – he

had amazingly skinny arms and legs for someone so, frankly, barrel-shaped.

'Why not?' I said. 'You scared or something?' Not that that would cut any ice with Tough-and-manly of the Welfare. Everyone learns to swim; it's a safety thing.

'I just don't want to. That's all.'

'So how did you square it with Welfare?'

'Welfare?' He grinned, like I'd said something really, really stupid. 'That was easy! The trick is, think logical. I asked whereabouts I was likely to come near any water deep enough to drown in.'

'You can drown in five centimetres if you're unconscious.'

'In that case, knowing how to swim wouldn't help any, would it? The only place within a thousand miles where the water's too deep to stand up in is right here in the pool. Logically, the safest thing is for me to stay away from the pool.'

'They bought that?'

'Why wouldn't they? It's been very simply programmed, you know.'

I frowned. 'What has?'

'The Welfare computer.'

'The what?' I stuck a finger in my ear and tried to shake some of the water out. I wasn't sure I was hearing this right. Sweet-as-sugar? Tough-and-manly? They were bits of a *computer*?

Sam shook his head. 'They're not real people,' he said, like he was telling a four-year-old that there's no Tooth fairy. 'Haven't you noticed it's always the same two voices?'

'Of course I've noticed!' I took a running dive back

into the pool and started swimming up and down like crazy while I tried to get this straight.

Do you know, it had never actually crossed my mind before that those two might not actually be real? Sweet-as-sugar. Tough-and-manly. Because, there always had been counsellors, ever since I could remember. You get sick, you call the doctor; any other problems, you call your counsellor. It still made me mad to think about it – if it was true! That they might have switched me into the less-than-loving care of a computer programme and never even bothered to tell me.

So I'd been having friendly little personal chats with a couple of personality chips? Sharing my innermost thoughts? Letting them solve my problems for me? Letting them run *my life*?

When I finally came up for air, Sam was right there by the pool, waiting for me: 'I wouldn't worry about it,' he said.

'I'm not worried.'

'The Company knows best.'

'Praise the Company.'

Irony was wasted on Sam. His smile spread wide: 'Yeah! All *right*! Let's go and get something to eat.'

That was the best idea he'd had yet.

It turned out to be not such a bad sort of day after all. I got a few odd looks, of course. Pairing up with a deek for the day is not considered normal. But who wants to be normal? And Sam had given me food for thought, as well as more than half his lunch.

Welfare was just a sophisticated computer programme. It made a kind of sense. Omega Seven was the perfect planet for perfect people; what could go wrong that a bit of logical thinking couldn't solve? They'd have to have some kind of human back-up, of course, the same way Maintenance did. I was still so busy pondering this whole business when I reached home, I clean forgot about my missing ID, and automatically passed my wrist over the scanner.

The door slid open.

I stepped inside, almost tripping over my own feet in my surprise, as I stared at my wrist. My ID bracelet had been there all the time.

No it hadn't; I'd got witnesses.

Whatever; it was here now. With rising hopes, I went over to the autocook and pressed a few buttons.

Curry.

Life is never that perfect.

While I was feeding what should have been my dinner into the waste disposal – *Want Not, Waste Not* – I heard the communicator whirring into action, as if it was clearing its throat. Followed by the voice of Sweet-as-sugar: 'Luke? Are you there?'

Of course. I was back on-line as soon as I used my ID.

'I'd like a word with you, Luke.'

'Oh, yes? Er. G'day.'

'Where have you been all day, Luke?'

OK, I thought, the first experiment – managing without my ID – that had worked. Let's try another one. Think logical.

'I've been at the Leisure Drome,' I said.

A pause. 'We have no record of your being there, Luke.'

'Well, that's where I was. I played chess with Sam,' I added helpfully.

Pause. 'Sam normally plays alone.'

'He played with me. Ask him. Ask anyone who was there. Plenty of people saw us. Then I went swimming.'

'Sam went swimming.'

'Sam never goes swimming.'

A longer pause, while she digested the contradictory facts so far: two people, not one, had played chess. Maybe. One of those two had checked out a pair of swimming-trunks. In Sam's favourite colour. That one couldn't be Sam, though – could it? – because Sam was excused swimming. In the end she decided to pass on that one. 'And where did you have breakfast?'

Better leave Pavel out of this. (I wasn't sure he was supposed to hoard food the way he did.)

'I ate at the Leisure Drome. I had to. There's nothing to eat here but curry.'

'Stay calm. Maintenance are sending a 'droid round in the morning.'

'You know that?'

'I know,' the voice said smugly, as if to say, 'We know everything.' But they didn't. They didn't! Not by a mile. I was almost sure now that Sam was right about the whole thing being a computer programme. I ran one final test: 'By the way,' I said.

'Yes, Luke?'

'As I was coming back from the Leisure Drome, I met a 'droid carrying a little green tripede on its shoulder. I said, "Where did you get that?" And the tripede said, "Well, it started out as this nasty wart on my behind."'

There was a heart-stopping pause. Then, 'This tripede spoke to you? In English?'

I breathed again. 'Of course not. It's a joke!'

'A joke. I see. Goodnight, Luke.'

'Goodnight,' I said.

All right, so it's an old joke, and not a very good one. But if Sweet-as-sugar had been human, at least she'd have understood it.

Another thought struck me. Wherever my ID had been, from the time it vanished from my wrist to the moment it magically reappeared, Welfare had got no record, no trace. None at all. They were no wiser than I was.

FIVE

The 'droid from Maintenance arrived first thing next morning to fix the autocook and Ma set off for the Bio Lab with a spring in her step and a tale to tell about the autocook that kept serving up curry. Maybe it didn't rate quite so high on the interest-scale as the cooker that vanished and came back Strangely Changed, but she got extra points for being the one it actually happened to.

Pavel was right; people need these stories.

There was more excitement in the air when I checked in at the school. People milling around in the main hall. Work-stations deserted.

'What's going on?' I asked the first person who'd stop to listen.

'General Assembly. You must have heard.'

'No.'

'Didn't you pick up your messages this morning?'

'Too busy.'

He gave me a disbelieving look. It was true. I'd been too absorbed in polishing up The Strange Case of the Disappearing ID for its first public performance to notice any flashing lights on the comm-Unit.

'Must be serious,' someone behind me said. 'They've even called the deeks in.'

'Look kind of spooky, don't they?' a third voice joined in. 'All of them together.'

The deeks were sitting silently, in neat rows, facing

front. I spotted Sam among them, tried to signal to him, give him the thumbs up, let him know that he'd been right about the Welfare. Fat chance. Forget it. Once back among his own kind, Sam didn't even glance my way.

So I turned to the three norms. 'A funny thing happened to me yesterday,' I began.

'Not now, Luke.'

'Save it for later.'

They were moving away.

I called after them, 'Hey, don't you want to hear this? This isn't a joke. This is serious.' But already they'd been swallowed up by the crowd. So I joined in the general shuffling about, groups forming and reforming, people changing their minds about who they wanted to sit with, until Mr Strangeways coasted in. And we all sat, dropping into the first available seat, like a game of Musical Chairs.

Mr Strangeways wasn't alone. Caught in his tractor-beam was this guy in Security-blue, about three metres tall with shoulders to match. There was a brief, optimistic, buzz of excitement, till it was clear that our Studies Supervisor was not, after all, under arrest. He ran through the usual spiel – today we have a visitor – listen carefully to what he has to say – give him every assistance.

Security-blue clasped his hands behind his back and looked us over with a glare that must have had many a raw recruit handing in his blaster and running home crying to his mother. We stared back, kind-of interested. All except the deeks. They just stared.

It's weird. You get this guy in a flash uniform, who's faced up to the Grammarian hoop-snake and the three-headed silica-beast of Hydra and played a star role in putting down the Robot Revolt of '79; you stand him in front of a bunch of school-kids, and suddenly he's jelly from the knees down. He opened his mouth to speak and what came out was 'Eek!'

We laughed.

Then you get Mr S. who'd have to call for back-up if he found a spider in the bath, and all he has to do is tuck in his chin – just so! – and raise his eyebrows – just so. You could have heard a pin drop.

Mr Blue cleared his throat and tried again. This time he came out with a full-bellied roar that set the windows humming in harmony: 'A CRIME has been committed.'

That got our attention. There was no crime on Omega Seven. Crime was one of the things we'd left behind us on Earth. I miss the old place. I really do.

'In the school,' he added, rubbing it in.

Eyes grew rounder. Mouths dropped open. We sat looking up at him like a shoal of stranded fish.

It got worse. Seems some hacker had been running amok in the school data-banks. Source-material, personal records, assignments half-completed . . . Files, or parts of files, popping up where they didn't belong. Re-classified, deleted, or cast into limbo . . . Computer-crime is as bad as it gets these days. Murder may earn you a life-sentence on one of the pioneer colonies, the Botany Bays. For assault on a computer, you get to have your brain cells re-arranged.

Then Mr Strangeways stepped forward again. 'It may be,' he said, casting an eagle eye over the usual suspects, 'that this is someone's idea of a *joke*.' For some reason his glance lit on me.

I shrugged. He turned away. I wouldn't have the know-how and he knew it.

He pressed on, with a regretful sigh, 'The only alternative explanation is that this was deliberate sabotage.' I could see why he might be getting edgy. Aside from Company head office, no-one had the kind of access to some of those files that allowed them to change a word of them except Mr Strangeways and the deputy, Mr Parkhurst.

'In which case' – he drew himself up defiantly – 'my message to the culprit is, 'You'll have to do better than that! Mr Parkhurst already has the virus under control. It may take a little longer to replace all of the missing files, but that will be no excuse for not completing an assignment on time. If you have any problems, ask for help.'

Then it was Mr Blue's turn again: 'If you've noticed anything unusual – anything at all! – during the last few days, or anyone acting strangely, we want to hear about it. Information will be dealt with in strictest confidence. There'll be an officer here on duty during school hours and a hot-line through to your home communications-units. The Company is depending on *you* to help us catch this – this—' We could feel him searching for the word that would sum up what he felt. 'This CRIMINAL!' he thundered.

There was a silence, bated breath all round, while everyone waited to see if anyone else was going to spill the beans. Then a collective sigh, half-relief, half-disappointment, followed by a murmuring and a muttering. You want unusual? We got it! You want strange? The whackier, the merrier. I started in with my story about my missing ID. But I was hardly off the mark when I was interrupted by a girl's voice, 'I lost a perfectly good football, much the same way. Put it down – turned round – turned back – and it was gone.'

'Yeah, I said, raising my voice a little, 'but my ID was actually on my wrist.'

'I found it, she went on, as if I hadn't spoken, 'days later, right where I'd left it. Turned totally inside-out. And I do mean totally!'

Someone else said, 'Let me tell you about this chess set of my pa's . . .' Got nowhere.

'Someone borrowed it,' a voice made itself heard over the murmuring all around.

'The football?'

'Put it back when they'd trashed it.'

'But it wasn't trashed!' the girl yelled back. 'What I'm saying is—'

'Yeah, but this whole chess set was there in the cupboard, so how come only the board went missing—'

'Put your hand up then, why don't you?'

'You mean, tell them about it?'

'He did say anything, however strange.'

'But this just sounds stupid.'

'Couldn't see for looking, if you ask me,' the kid beside me grinned.

'It was still playable with – but inside out. Is that weird or what?'

'But I *was* looking!' I insisted. 'I'd just checked the time.' The school clown, that's me. A joke for all occasions. So now I'm being serious for once, no-one's listening. 'I'm *telling* you. The ID was there on my wrist. Then it was gone. All day almost. When I got home, it was there on my wrist again. How do you explain that? Look, this could be important! Will somebody listen to me? Please?'

'We are listening, Luke,' Mr Strangeways said quietly, fixing me with an oh-not-you-again look. I realised I'd been the only one still talking.

'Speak up, Luke,' he said. 'If you've got something helpful to say, let's all hear it.'

I shrank to about ten centimetres tall. 'I was only saying,' I said weakly, 'that I thought I'd lost my ID yesterday and then it was suddenly there again, on my wrist.'

'Are you suggesting that the missing files may have simply been – overlooked?'

Think positive; that's my motto. 'They'll probably turn up,' I said. 'Things do, don't they?'

'That's your advice, is it? That we should all sit back and wait for the missing files to Turn Up? And the files which appear to have been deliberately vandalised?'

I said carefully, 'Are you sure it's a hacker? That it wasn't just a blip on the control-comp?'

'A BLIP!' You could have sliced through tungsten with that *blip*! I let it go, in spite of the dutiful sniggering all around. I got my revenge. No-one volunteered any information of any sort after that, for fear of looking equally stupid.

I was busy turning things over in my mind. What happened to the school computer was so like the story of the vanishing autocook (files down-loaded, turned inside out, shuffled around and fed back in all anyhow), Security must have made a connection. If the autocook story was true. And what about our autocook, getting stuck on curry? They'd have that information too, by now, keyed in to Cen-trol by MainTech One – another good reason for me to keep a low profile.

What they didn't have was the full story of my disappearing ID. I'd tried to tell them, hadn't I? They'd had their chance. Not my fault they wouldn't listen. I couldn't quite see how it fitted in with the rest, but maybe – just maybe – I held the missing piece that would make sense of the whole puzzle. What if I could solve the mystery, when Security and everyone else was baffled? Then, maybe, they'd have to take me seriously. No more Mr Jokey-Cool! Let's have a little respect around here.

I had to talk to Pavel, soonest. Kept myself in check all day and went straight to the Science Block after school, but Pavel wasn't around. The tripede didn't seem to be short of food, so I guessed he'd been back and gone out again.

Went home and tried to sleep, ideas spinning round in my head. Things going missing. Systems scrambled. Could it be something in the air, maybe? The same thing that made the Blue Mountain seem close one day, far off the next. Some undiscovered gas! A gas that could make you not see something that was really there? Mess up computer circuits too?

I gave up on that one first thing next day, as soon as I heard that Mr Strangeways had gone missing. The image of Mr Strangeways as the Invisible Man, wandering around, in or out of his night-clothes, was one I didn't want to contemplate.

Mrs Strangeways was very upset about it. Welfare tried to persuade her to Stay Calm.

'Stay calm,' they told her. 'There's nothing on Omega Seven that can hurt him.'

'Stay calm!' screeched Mrs Strangeways. She would not stay calm. They might stay calm if they liked, if their partner for the last twenty years had vanished from beside them in the middle of the night.

'Stay calm,' they said. He'd probably slipped out on his own, remembering something he'd forgotten to do – at the school, most likely.

And how was he going to get in there or anywhere else without his ID, demanded Mrs Strangeways, brandishing it.

They searched high and they searched low and found not one trace. Mr Strangeways did seem to have disappeared right out of the Colony. And if he'd wanted to go into the disappearing business, snapped Mrs Strangeways, he needn't have come halfway across the galaxy to do it. He could have signed up as a conjurer's assistant in a travelling circus. Welfare gave up trying to pacify her and quietly moved her into quarantine, just in case the bad vibes turned out to be catching.

And if you're wondering how I knew all this, I just did. Everyone did. It was too good a story for it not to get around.

They called in the geology teams from the Outlands and all but essential staff from the experimental farms and the mines, closed off the main gate and upped the strength of the force-field round the Colony.

Still no sign of Pavel. He must be on an extended field-trip. He wasn't Company, so they weren't worried. I worried about him for a bit. Not for long. If the last recorded sighting of Mr Strangeways was inside the colony, then outside ought to be the safer place to be. Or at least *as* safe. At least, I hoped so.

* * *

Looked like I was on my own for a while. I started trying to get my thoughts on the investigation into some sort of order. Think like Pavel, I told myself. How would Pavel go about this? First of all, he'd say, only trust the data which you know to be true.

So what had I got? An autocook serving up curry three times a day and nothing but. An ID bracelet that vanished and then came back again. And the hacking into the school computer, which I'd got no first-hand knowledge of, but I guessed it must be true.

And should I add in what I'd discovered about the Welfare? About it being all on computer? OK, I know Sam told me first. But I'd found my own way of checking it. Maybe that wasn't part of the main problem, but useful to know. I placed it in a mental sub-file, to call up again if necessary.

So what had I got? Two machines acting strange (three, if I added in the vanishing autocook); one disappearance and re-appearance (two, if I added in the vanishing autocook; three, if I added in Mr Strangeways – if he came back again. Think positive, I told myself. He'd be back.) Not enough. I desperately needed more information. So I hunted down the girl who'd been going on about the football that turned inside out.

'That football of yours—'

'What football?'

'Can I see it?'

'It's just a football.'

I turned it over and over in my hands. It was just a football. 'I thought you said it turned totally inside out?'

'Why would it do that?'

'I don't know, but you said—'

'When did I say that?'

'But still playable with.'

'Anyway, it's not possible.' She snatched it back. 'You're weird, you know that?'

She'd been got at, I decided. Security, Welfare, her own Ma and Pa afraid of being sent back Earthside? What difference did it make?

The kid with the chessboard – the one that vanished from out of a locked cupboard, remember? – he was more helpful. But not much.

'Oh yes,' he said. 'It came back again. About two days later. Thanks for asking.'

'Was the cupboard still locked?'

He nodded.

'Can I see?'

He shook his head. 'Pa still thinks it was me. That's his luxury item, you see. The chess set.' I nodded, understanding. Everyone gets one luxury item they can bring from Earth, plus a favourite book. Kids tend to grow out of them after about six months, but grown-ups can get really attached. 'He says if I lay a finger on it again, he'll get me sent to the dormitories.' Pause. 'He wouldn't, though, would he?'

'Course not.' Still, I didn't want to be responsible.

I pinned my hopes on Mr Strangeways turning up again, which ought to tell me something, though I wasn't sure what. And he did, as suddenly as he'd gone. Mr Parkhurst came into school one morning and found Mr Strangeways sitting on the floor in his nightclothes, a Security officer's cap perched backwards on his head. He kept muttering to himself:

'It's no good1 I can't do it! I don't *understand*!'

Mr P sent for Security, who hauled out Mr S, then sent for the medics, who gave him hot drinks, bathed him and tranquillised him and put him to bed. The minute he came round, Security were there, on the spot, asking him where he'd been.

'I don't know,' he said. 'It doesn't make sense! I can't work it out. I must work it out!'

'Work what out?'

He shook his head. 'I can't explain.'

Stick to the easy stuff: 'Where – Have – You – Been?'

'I don't know.'

'Tell us about it.'

He sighed and shook his head: 'You wouldn't believe me. I don't believe it myself! And I was *there*!' He blinked: 'Wasn't I?'

In the end, Welfare booked the Strangewayses, Mr and Mrs, two one-way tickets to the Happy Planet and put Mr Parkhurst in charge of studies. He promptly declared a general rest-day, so we could all make a fresh start. Like twenty-four hours would be long enough to wipe The Mysterious Disappearance of Mr Strangeways clean out of our minds.

I *had* to talk to Pavel.

The gate was open again and Pavel had come strolling back in, apparently knowing nothing about all the fuss that had been going on while he was away. I wasn't too sure that he'd want to be out and about again so soon. But he had promised – hadn't he? – the next free day I had, he'd take me with him to the Blue Mountain. And while we were out there, we could talk this whole thing through, without being overheard or interrupted.

I rushed through breakfast and down to the Science Block. Checked in with no more than the usual amount of hassle. Ran downstairs to the ecology lab, afraid he might have already gone without me.

'Pavel!' I called.

From inside, as I struggled, as usual, to push open the door, I heard Sam's voice: 'Hi, Luke!'

'What's he doing here?' I said, as I finally forced an entry.

'Looking for you, I think,' said Pavel.

'We're going to the Blue Mountain!' crowed Sam, triumphant.

We? As in 'we three'? If it had been any other place, I'd have said I was busy. But the thought of Sam getting there before me . . . And Pavel was already loading us both up with bits of equipment to carry. I followed the two of them upstairs and waited with Sam for Pavel to bring the hovercar round.

'You found your ID again then?' said Sam.

'I never said I lost it.'

Silence.

'I can come if I want,' said Sam. 'Dr Pavlov's not your property, you know.'

Not being able to think of a suitable put-down, I kept a dignified silence.

I made sure I was first inside the hovercar. Which turned out to be a mistake, since the car only had two doors. I had to squeeze in the back, along with Pavel's equipment, when Sam scrambled in after me. So it was Sam who got to ride in the front.

SIX

We were going to the Blue Mountain! I kept reminding myself how much I'd looked forward to it before. That gut-churning feeling when I flashed my ID for the guard at the gate and there it was – not! The disappointment as I stood watching the car hi-tailing it across the plain.

No problem this time. We were through the gate and on our way. And all I could feel was annoyed. Annoyed at Sam's head plonked in front of me, blocking half the view.

Even half that view, though, is quite something. You keep trying to shoehorn what you see into what you know, but the whole place is topsy-turvy. There are rocks and hills and streams, the same as on Earth, but the nearest thing to grass is a sort of undulating sea-blue moss. No trees, but giant ferns, like in the time of the dinosaurs, and stuff like clusters of monstrous seaweed, brown and green and rusty-red, turning itself face-on to the sun, mornings and evenings, edge-on in the heat of the day, to stop itself being burned to a frazzle. Six-legged creatures, knee-high to an elephant, hoovering up the dust between with their trunks. Swaying high above are sort-of mushrooms, thin stems vibrating in the wind, giving off a faint humming sound. There's one tiny creature that spends its whole life crawling up those stems, feeding on the patches of mould – whatever – that grow there. When it gets to the top, it lays its eggs and dies. The eggs float down to the ground, where they hatch, and the young ones begin the long crawl up again. For them, the entire Meaning of Life is making it to the top of a giant mushroom.

'Look!' cried Pavel.

Down a hillside, ahead and to our right, a shimmering ball came tumbling, faster and faster. Just when we thought the car was bound to hit it, the ball lifted off the ground and spread out, thin and iridescent as a butterfly's wing, but two metres across at least, and, riding the thermals, soared away into the sky.

Sam turned his head when he was told to look at something; then turned back to face the front, saying nothing, as if he'd seen it all before. So I played it cool, too. Inside I was finding it all pretty amazing. Life, eh? All the different forms of it. Amazing.

Slowly the Blue Mountain towered up in front of us until it blotted out the sky. Like a solid wall, rippling with a squillion shades of blue, as the light sparked off jutting outlines or turned to almost-black inside deep folds and crevices. Not a living thing growing on it, anywhere. Not a pocket of dust blown in from the land around, where plants could gain a foothold. I'd never expected it to be quite this big.

The car slowed, settled and stopped.

Pavel said, 'You are quiet today, you two.'

'Sorry,' said Sam. 'Hovercars always make me feel a bit sick.'

'Get out, then,' he said, 'and walk around. Take a little air. Soon you'll be OK.'

No-one asked me how I felt, bundled up in the

back, like a piece of surplus luggage.

Then I got out, stretching my legs, close enough to rub shoulders with the Blue Mountain for the first time. Magic! I put out my hand and felt the glassy surface, warm from the sun, shades of blue rippling and changing as cloud-shadows moved across, almost as if the mountain was alive and breathing.

'Harder than diamonds!' I murmured under my breath. 'Blasters – lasers – plasma bolts haven't so much as left a mark.'

'Perhaps they've been going about it the wrong way.' That was Sam, making a miracle-recovery from his motion-sickness. 'Trying to force a way through, I mean,' he said.

'You mean we should ask it nicely?' I raised my voice: 'Hey, mister! Let us through, will you?'

Pavel, busy adjusting his recording equipment a short distance away, looked up and grinned. Glad to see the two of us getting on so well together. Even Pavel didn't get things right all the time.

'*I* wouldn't let you in,' Sam said primly. 'Not if you yelled at me like that.'

I was watching the tripedes. There were dozens of them here, all rushing about like keep-fit freaks. And then . . . First one – I didn't believe it the first time, so I kept a close eye on them, until another – then another! – ran straight up to the mountainside and vanished into it. They just kept going, as if it wasn't there.

'Maybe,' I murmured, half-joking, 'all we need is the magic word. Like, Open Sesame. And we'd find ourselves on the other side of the mountain, in a magical, hidden valley. Shangri-la.' My mind was still focused on the tripedes, the way they just kept going. Remembering that one Pavel kept in his lab trying to walk through the wall of glass. As if all it had to do was believe the glass wasn't there. 'Open Sesame,' I murmured again, my hand still resting against the rock-wall. And slowly, right before my very eyes, my hand began disappearing into the wall. As if the rock was no more solid than water.

I shut my eyes.

When I opened them again, I was standing at the foot of a sheer cliff-wall, staring out at a scene that was like nothing anywhere on Omega Seven. A bare, mountain landscape, studded with rocks and stones. Dust underfoot. Rough grass. Dry shrubs. Behind me, a grey wall of rock, crumbling in places. But I knew for a fact the Blue Mountain had been explored on the far side and shown nothing but the same sheer face of glassy blue.

Where was I, then? Inside the mountain? But all the scans had shown the Blue Mountain was solid, through and through. Some hidden crater? Above me, I could see the sky, but it was looking all wrong, lowering grey, with storm clouds scudding across it. A cold wind whipped up the dust around my legs.

'Luke?' I heard Sam's voice, muffled by the rock. 'Luke! Where are you? Where did you go?'

'I'm here.'

'Where's here?'

I swallowed hard. 'That hidden valley we were just talking about? Shangri-la? I think I just found it.'

'You what?'

'All I said was Open Sesame.'

'Open Sesame?' echoed back through the rock. A little way along from me, the cliff-wall bellied outwards and the bulge turned into Sam, eyes closed, arms held out in front of him, like a sleepwalker.

He opened his eyes, blinked once, dropped his arms to his sides and looked around. 'Oh wow! This looks just like . . .' He stopped and shook his head, as if to clear it. Then he looked at me, like I had some way of knowing what he was thinking. 'With the hills around – and that track down there – if the sun was shining, I'd say we were—'

'We were where?' I said.

'A place we went. Just before I got posted. The shape of that rock over there . . . like an enormous cat – see, there's the tail. But it can't be.' He blinked and rubbed his eyes, turned round once, then looked again. 'Actually,' he said, 'it's nothing like it.'

I can't say I wasn't relieved to have company, but the first shock was beginning to wear off. This could be interesting. 'Come on,' I said. 'Let's take a look around.'

'I think we ought to go back,' Sam said nervously.

'Not yet! Come on! What's to be scared of?'

He stood hesitating. 'We'd better tell Dr Pavlov where we're going.' He turned to the cliff-face, put his hands up against it and pushed. He called out, 'Open Sesame!'

Nothing happened.

'You try,' he said.

I stepped up to the rock. I pressed my palms up against it, willing it to let me through. 'Open Sesame!' I shouted.

Nothing.

'It doesn't work from this side,' said Sam. He sounded scared. I was feeling a little panicky myself.

'Let's try it backwards,' I suggested. 'Sesame Open? Er'

– trying to visualise the words written down – 'emases nepo!'

'Dr Pavlov!' Sam was yelling now. 'Where was he, Luke? Over to our left?'

'Right. Both together now! Pavel!'

'Dr Pavlov!'

We shouted together and kept on shouting. It wasn't till we both stopped for breath that we heard Pavel calling back: 'Stay calm, you two! I hear you! But I can't see you.'

'We're inside!'

'On the other side!'

'We don't know where we are.'

'We can't get back.'

'Stay calm. I'll find you. How did you get in there?'

Sam answered, 'We just said—'

'Don't say it!' I yelled.

'—Open Sesame,' Sam finished.

Already Pavel was taking shape in front of us, part of the rock wall, then separate, a look of complete bewilderment on his face. 'Remarkable! I think I have just walked through a solid wall,' he said. 'Am I a ghost?' Then he took in the view. He gave a low whistle. 'This is like the Earth, new made, before there were people in every corner. It's beautiful.'

Sam pointed. 'But there's a road down there. See. Running down that slope to our left, then skirting the bottom of the hill we're standing on.'

A road? Looked more like a rough track to me – if that. The thought floated through my mind that we seemed to be seeing three slightly different things. What I said aloud was, 'There doesn't seem to be any way back.'

Pavel thought for a moment, running his hand over the cliff-face. Then he said, 'This is no longer the Blue Mountain. This is rock like you find on Earth. There will be places where it is less steep to climb. We'll find a way up and over. Come on. It is getting too cold anyway, for standing about.'

SEVEN

The wind blew icy cold. A thick cloud-layer covered the sky and the light was fading fast. Pavel was right: dressed for a warm Omega Seven day, this was no time to be standing about wondering what this place was.

We moved along, exploring every fissure in the rock, searching for a spot where it might be possible to climb up, trying all the time to keep close to the foot of the cliffs, but rock-falls and dense scrub steered us further and further away. Deep down inside, I think I knew it wasn't going to be that easy.

At length Pavel called a halt. 'This is no good,' he said. 'I think, maybe we should go back and try the other way. Are you all right, Sam?'

Sam said, 'Listen!'

At first I thought it was just the wind, but then I heard it too. The sound of whistling. A lot of men, whistling in chorus. And the tramp of marching feet, coming closer.

Without anyone saying the word – 'Duck!' – we ducked down out of sight behind the rocks as they came into view.

The leader – with the hook-nose and the temper of one of the nastier birds of prey, if faces are anything to go by – was on horseback. The rest marched on foot, in ranks of four, led by a standard bearer with a leopard skin, head and all, trailing down his back. Shirts, kilts and breeches, all blood-red, with brass helmets and body armour, plus swords, spears, daggers and shields. There was a mean, dogged look about them. They were whistling because they'd been ordered to; not because they were happy. They didn't look like the sort of people who'd take kindly to someone strolling out from among the rocks to say, 'Excuse me! Can you tell us the way back to the Colony?'

Out of the misty twilight they came marching, while we crouched in the cover of the rocks. Into the gathering gloom they vanished again. The whistling died away.

Pavel had taken off his glasses and was polishing them like they'd never been polished before. There was a gleam of excitement in his eyes.

'This is fascinating,' he said. 'Did we all see the same thing?'

Good point.

'I saw—'

'Romans,' whispered Sam.

'Roman *soldiers*,' I chipped in. 'Centurion, standard bearer and all. What's the matter, Sam?'

'You saw the standard.' His skin had turned a sickly shade of pale beneath the brown. 'They were the Ninth Legion. In the year one-hundred-and-something the Ninth Legion marched north out of England to fight against the Brigantes.'

'The who?'

'The Brigantes. Doesn't matter. The point is, the Ninth Legion were never seen again. Not a trace.'

'So, what are you suggesting? They were abducted by aliens? Or maybe they just kept marching? And somehow wound up here! Get real, Sam!'

He stood his ground, though his teeth were chattering, only partly from cold. 'As s-soon as I s-saw the way the r-r-road was paved, I knew it would be R-r-romans.'

'Paved?' I slid down the slope to check it out, so I could prove him wrong. But Sam was right. What I'd taken at first sight to be a rough, barely discernible track turned out to be your classic Roman road, neatly cambered and paved with cobblestones. Marking the way the men had gone was a steaming pile of horse dung, which put paid to any thoughts I might have had about this being some kind of elaborate hologram. Besides, what about the weather?

As I scrambled back up the slope, I could hear Sam's voice, 'Let's g-g-go after them. Whoever they were, they'll have a f-f-fire, and shelter.'

The cold was clearly getting to his brain. I said, 'The only shelter those guys would have to offer is the sort where the doors can only be opened from the outside. You could see it in their faces.'

'They d-d-didn't look that b-b-bad to me,' Sam argued.

Pavel, crouching down, picking over some of the dead sticks lying around, said, 'I think Luke is right. Until we know who these people are, we should keep clear of them if we can.' He glanced up at the sky. Heavy clouds were gathered so low you could almost reach up and touch them. 'First things first. We must find somewhere to shelter, out of the cold.' Even as he spoke, the first fat snowflakes began to idle downwards. 'A dry cave.' He cast an eye around. 'There!' he pointed.

And there it was. The perfect shelter. With ivy training

decoratively round the entrance. All that was missing was the Welcome mat.

'And now,' said Pavel, once we were inside, 'we must get ourselves warm again. Find a way of making fire. Here is plenty of dry wood.'

'How are you going to light it?' I asked.

'By rubbing two sticks together. As cave dwellers must have done in the old days.' Trying to make it sound like fun. So I played along. Set off to collect all the dry wood I could lay my hands on. From the first armful I brought back, he picked out a flattish block and using his old pocket knife – the one with blades for everything, that he got from his grandpa – he hacked a rough groove out of one side. Then, selecting a different blade, he began gouging a socket in the middle of the block. 'Kindling!' he grunted, the moment I hunkered down to watch. 'I must have kindling. Dry moss. Grasses. Pine needles. Fungi. All very dry.'

So, off I went again. When I came back, Pavel had twined together a cord and tied it to a pliable length of stick to make a bow. He was just finishing sharpening a straight hardwood stake into a rough point at either end.

'Now!' he said. 'I have seen this in books, but never tried it. I'm not sure I have enough hands!'

'Let me help.'

He shook his head, but he let me stay to watch. Using his feet to hold the wood block steady, he fixed his pointed stick upright in the socket and packed a fistful of dry moss loosely round it. Then he took the makeshift bow in his right hand and looped the string once round the upright, holding it in place with another, smaller, flat piece of wood held in his left hand, resting it on top.

'Fingers crossed. Ready?'

I nodded.

'Steady – Go!' He began sawing away with the bow, which set the upright spinning, producing a fine-brown-black trickle of sawdust. I caught a smell of scorching.

I could see it now! A tiny wisp of smoke, coiling up from the socket. Pavel bent to blow gently at the little pile of kindling.

'You've done it!' I yelled.

The smoke gave a silent hiccup and disappeared.

'Sorry,' I said.

'Not your fault.' Pavel began sawing away again like crazy. The upright was a blur. 'Fetch me more twigs!' he commanded, without slowing down. 'Very thin. We must have more twigs or the fire will die!'

Snow was falling thickly now, damping the dead wood lying about in the open faster than I could collect it. I was moving further from the cave, grubbing about under the bushes, to find the really dry stuff. Rooting about in a really thick patch of undergrowth, I caught sight of a pair of eyes watching me.

The face was in deep shadow. All I could make out was the eyes, shining, unblinking. Something inside me – maybe my stomach lurching, like on a roller-coaster – told me that the owner wasn't human.

Stay calm, I told myself. There's nothing on Omega Seven than can hurt you.

'Go 'way!' I said aloud, flapping a hand towards whatever-it-was.

Whatever-it-was didn't go away. It raised a hairy arm and waved back.

I panicked and ran, scattering wood in all directions,

and didn't stop till I was back inside the cave. I crouched by Pavel and told him what I had seen: some kind of creature, watching me.

He didn't turn a hair. He was still totally focused on the fire, which was now a cheerfully crackling pile of twigs, none of them thicker than my finger. 'There is another of them over to the left,' he said. 'Also watching us.'

'Why?' I demanded.

Pavel answered placidly, 'You can learn a lot by watching. Maybe even the secret of how to make fire.'

He reached over to balance a thicker branch on the burning twigs. Bent his head close to the ground and puffed gently. The branch caught, burning brighter, flames licking upwards. I could feel the warmth of it on my legs. Beyond the tiny flickering circle of firelight it suddenly seemed very dark.

'Where is Sam?' asked Pavel.

'I'm here,' said Sam, creeping closer to the fire from deep in the cave where he'd been skiving while I fetched in the wood. The exercise would have done him good. Kept him warm. Taken his mind off things.

'Did you see them?' he asked.

Pavel answered calmly, 'I have seen them.'

EIGHT

The fire was going well now. The three of us huddled close to it, keeping our faces to the cave entrance and the clearing beyond. First one, then the other of the creatures edged into the growing circle of firelight. And there they sat, keeping each other company.

'What do they want?' I muttered. 'What are they doing here?'

Pavel smiled. 'Watching us. Studying. Observing.'

'You talk as if they were human.'

'What would you call them? Animals? Our earliest ancestors looked very much like them, I guess.'

Suddenly the burning twigs gave way, a log fell and a shower of sparks flew upwards. Both creatures leapt into the air and came down clutching one another for support. It was a while before one of them plucked up the courage to let go, and began edging forwards again.

I picked up a stone. 'Go away!' I yelled.

It flapped a hand at me in friendly fashion and shuffled closer.

I stood up, stepped back and threw the stone – not to hit it, just frighten it off.

Dust flew up round the creature's feet.

It stopped.

The other ape-man hunkered over, picked up the stone and lobbed it back, catching me on the shin.

It hurt. This was no virtual reality trip. That stone was

real. So was the blood. Pavel said nothing, just passed me a hunk of moss to mop up the worst of it. When I looked up again, the two creatures had gone.

'I think, maybe, that was not such a smart thing to do, Luke,' Pavel said quietly.

'Why not?'

The snow was falling fast, drifting up against the rocks and bushes, but the fire was blazing merrily and we were warm at last. For answer, he just pointed. The ape-men were back, and this time they'd brought their friends and relations with them.

'Always begin by trying to make friends. You haven't learnt this in school? Only if the other party attacks, should you strike back.'

'I didn't mean to hit them.'

'They didn't know that. They were two and we were three. If we had offered to make friends when the odds were in our favour . . . Never mind.'

The ape-men sat all round the edges of the clearing. The snow settled on their heads, shoulders and feet, dressing them in uniform: peaked caps, epaulettes and fluffy bedroom slippers. I felt sorry for them sitting there, just beyond the warmth of the fire. Not sorry enough, though, to invite them in.

'What do we do?' I murmured.

Pavel, one eye on the cavemen and the other on the fire, murmured, 'The fire won't keep them off for long. So! Looks like our choice now is to fight or run away. I think they are too many to fight, but where can we run to?'

The flames were dying. I would never have believed how fast wood can burn away to nothing. 'Pity we don't have any coal,' mused Pavel. 'Coal burns hotter, longer . . .'

The creatures began edging nearer, shuffle, shuffle, stop. Look. Wait.

'I can feel a draught,' came Sam's voice, echoing hollowly from the back of the cave. 'I said, I can feel a draught. Back here. But it's too dark. I can't see properly.' He sniffed noisily. 'It smells like fresh air, but I can't see where it's coming from. If we could get a bit of light back here . . .'

'I'm coming,' murmured Pavel. He plucked a branch from the fire, puffed gently at it till the flames glowed steadily, then backed away into the cave to investigate.

I was left alone, facing the creatures. The aliens? I didn't want to get close enough to find out what they were. I didn't dare turn my back. Behind me, I heard Pavel's voice: 'Looks like a fissure leading back into the rock.'

Then Sam. 'Where do you think it goes to?'

Pavel again: 'The air is fresh. But the way may become too steep for us, or too narrow.'

I whispered: 'Pavel. The fire's going out. What do I do?'

'I think we must take this chance that is offered to us. Pile on the rest of the wood. But carefully. Make sure to get it blazing. Then quickly join us.'

I did as I was told. Stoked the fire, one piece at a time, with every last splinter of wood. Then backed away from the closing semi-circle of patient faces.

Pavel slithered through first, taking the torch with him, a faint flicker of light to show us the way.

Sam went next.

Then, with a nervous glance over my shoulder towards the last starry burst of fire, me.

On the far side, the fissure soon widened out into a passageway, not high enough even for Sam to stand upright, but wide-ish, leading deep into the heart of the mountain.

We didn't talk much as we went along; it's not easy to talk when you're bent almost double, trying to hurry. We couldn't be sure the ape-men didn't know about this place and wouldn't follow. Though the chances were they were as frightened of the dark as they were of fire.

How long before the torch went out, leaving us in total blackness?

Shadows danced around us, tall, short, leaping ahead or crouching behind, briefly lighting the entrances to low tunnels leading away into the deeper dark. The place was like a honeycomb.

No sounds of anyone following.

Gradually the roof sloped higher until I could stand upright without bumping my head. We began moving faster. I called out to Pavel: 'What is this place? It's not just an ordinary cave.'

Over his shoulder he called back, 'Some kind of mine, I think.'

'One of ours?'

He ran a quick hand over the wall. 'Not one of ours. This was dug out by hand.'

'Romans?' suggested Sam.

'Not Romans, I think.' In the dim light Pavel peered at his smudged fingers, sniffed at them. 'This seems to be a coal mine. In a coal mine, there will be people.'

Now he came to mention it, I could near them. Murmur of voices, whispering. What sounded like the snatch of a song. The steady beat of hammers and pickaxes, followed by a rumble of falling rocks. Could be a mile away, or just around the corner. We saw no-one.

'Soon!' Pavel kept saying, to keep our spirits up. 'Soon we will find someone who will tell us the way out of here.'

Suddenly, rounding a corner, we came upon a sort of someone. A little kid sitting cross-legged. It was wearing a pair of ragged shorts, a bowler hat with a stub of lighted candle stuck to the front and a thick coating of coal dust. It stared at us with red-rimmed eyes, saying nothing, pulling rhythmically on a string that worked a canvas flap that moved a stream of cool air down the tunnel.

Pavel crouched down beside it. 'You speak English?' he asked.

The kid said nothing, just carried on pulling on its string, but we got the impression it had understood.

'Can you tell us where we are?' he asked it.

'We're here,' it said.

'Where is here?'

'Down the mine o'course.'

'What is up there?' Pavel asked, pointing.

The kid followed the direction of his finger. 'The roof,' it said. Then it tugged hard once on the string and stopped. The canvas flap stayed up. The kid sat waiting for us to go through. 'Go on, then. Straight on till morning. You can't miss it.'

'Come with us,' I said.

The kid turned and looked down the tunnel into the dark, and shook its head so hard it nearly put its candle out. So we ducked past and walked on, leaving it sitting there, feeling the cool air wafting after us.

'I still think we should have asked those Romans for help,' fretted Sam. 'They'd have had hot baths – and central heating—'

'And nasty ways of dealing with people who weren't Romans,' I put in. 'Like throwing them to the lions!'

Sam came right back at me, 'The Romans were civilised. Organised! They built roads and towns and proper houses. They brought civilisation to the barbarians.'

'Whether they wanted roads and towns and Romans bossing them about, or not.'

'After the Romans there was a thousand years of the Dark Ages. You wouldn't have wanted to live in the Dark Ages, I bet. Nobody would. Not even the people who lived there, except they didn't know any better.'

'So roll on the Middle Ages.'

'The Middle Ages was rubbish, too. All they did was build castles and fight each other.'

'Castles, great! Four good, thick walls, keeping your rotten Romans out! I'll settle for that!'

'Sh! you two,' hissed Pavel. 'I think we're finally getting somewhere.'

Just as the torch finally guttered and went out, we came to a dead end. A place where seven tunnels met, all identical. Turn round once and you'd be hard put to recognise the way you came in. Far above I could see a small, round patch of inky sky and a scattering of stars. Night-time already? I couldn't believe we'd been walking that long.

'Our way out,' Pavel announced.

'You think so?' I said.

'I'm sure of it.'

'We can't climb up there!' groaned Sam.

'We can't stay here,' I pointed out.

'Perhaps there's another way.' He'd have been off down the nearest tunnel if I hadn't grabbed him.

'Listen!' I said. 'I can hear voices. People.'

'People?' said Sam.

I said: 'Who do you think they are?'

'There's only one way to find out,' Pavel announced, a bit over-cheerfully, to my mind.

NINE

Pavel felt around for a bit and found a set of iron rungs, up around shoulder-height. 'I will go first,' he said. He swung himself up and began to climb. After a while, he stopped and called quietly down, 'It's not so hard! Come on, Sam. You next.'

Before Sam could argue, 'I'll give you a bunk-up,' I said. I made a stirrup with my hands and grabbed his foot. A quick one, two three, heave-ho! and he was on his way.

I followed close on his heels. The going wasn't difficult. Even when the rungs gave out, it was no harder than the rock wall in the Leisure Drome. The difference was that in the Leisure Drome you have full safety gear and something soft to fall on. Sam would just have me. It gave the whole experience an extra edge, believe me.

Pavel kept saying things like: 'It's OK, Sam. You're doing fine. Just watch where I put my hands and feet. Don't look down. Luke is watching your feet.'

You bet! Sam still kept missing his footing. He'd give a yelp and his leg would go rigid, so I had to slap it hard before he'd let me steer it back on course.

Above us, the stars began to fade, one by one until, glancing up, I could see that it was still daylight after all. Blue sky. The odd fluffy, white cloud floating by, going nowhere special.

'I'm *sure* I can hear people,' I said.

'I hear them too,' Pavel answered quietly.

'Is it the Romans?' asked Sam.

Pavel clambered the last few feet and peered cautiously over the top. 'Not Romans.' He vanished over the edge.

A hand came down, caught hold of Sam and hauled him up and out of sight. By the time the hand appeared again, I'd scrambled high enough to grab it. Too late I realised it wasn't Pavel's hand I was holding. Too leathery. I felt myself lifted into the air, blinking in the sunlight, barking my shin as I tumbled over a low, rough stone wall, so the blood started oozing again.

A voice said, 'IDs, please.'

Sounded like we'd arrived.

As I scrambled to my feet, I took a swift look around. And I thought to myself, Hey! maybe I'd inherited a smidgeon of Pa's talent for telepathy after all. First of all half-knowing, half-guessing about the hidden valley beyond the Blue Mountain. Shangri-la. And how to get to it. Open Sesame! And now . . . Why would I have suddenly started talking about castles – of all things! – if somewhere, somehow, at the back of my mind, I didn't know we were going to end up standing in the courtyard of what had to be a dead ringer for a medieval castle?

'ID, please,' said the voice again. The owner of the leathery hands. He had that seen-it-all-heard-it-all-before look of guards everywhere. There was a standard-issue scanner clipped to his belt, and he knew how to use it. But in place of the Company uniform, I saw battered leather and unwashed homespun, with a fits-all-sizes grey, knitted vest over the top.

'You took your time,' the guard remarked, as he scanned my ID. 'Everything all right down there?'

Pavel answered casually, 'Fine. No problem.'

'No problem!' I echoed.

Sam had switched to deek-mode. On autopilot. I took another look around.

It *was* a castle. I'd been quite heavily into castles at one time. Spent hours in front of my 3D-U, running through different siege scenarios. Silently I rolled the old familiar words around on my tongue. The courtyard we were standing in was called the bailey. That huge grille door was the portcullis, beyond which stood the barbican, or gatehouse. Crenellations, that was the up-and-down shape of the battlements. The up-bits were merlons. The in-between bits were the embrasures. The walkway behind was called the allure. Maybe, later on, we could take the guided tour . . . What was I thinking of? This was Omega Seven. This castle had no business to be here, any more than a bunch of Romans or a tribe of Neanderthals . . .

'Take cover!' the guard said suddenly. 'This way! Come on!' And he shot off. Sam followed, deek-wise, matching his speed to the person in front. I had to hand it to Pavel as he strolled after them. He was Mr Supercool. Totally unfazed. Looking casually around. Taking things in one at a time. Sniffing the air. Reaching for the notebook and pencil he always carried somewhere about him.

The guard stopped within a whisker of the wall and spun round to face us. There was something strangely familiar about that face. Rugged, dependable.

'Come on, Luke!' he sang out. 'Hurry, hurry, hurry!'

I urged my legs, still aching from the climb, into a shambling trot. As soon as I caught up, I asked him, 'Do I know you?'

He said, 'Do you?'

'Have you got a brother who works in Maintenance?'

'Maintenance?' He squinted up at me, dead-pan: 'Where's that? Is it far from here?'

'Maintenance! MainTech One?'

He shook his head.

'Forget it,' I said.

'Right,' he said. 'I will.' He turned his face upwards and scanned the sky, like he was looking for the first sign of rain. I leaned against the castle wall, enjoying the afternoon sunlight, the dust-free air and the warmth of the stonework on my back, and took a more leisurely look around.

The castle wasn't just four plain, stone walls. There were buildings of all shapes and sizes nestling up against them. Tucked in between were stacks of barrels and bales of hay. Mounds of rubbish. Lines of washing, strung out to dry. A scatter of abandoned cooking fires with the smoke still curling upwards, cauldrons bubbling and grid-irons smouldering. Where were all the people? Earlier on we'd heard voices, movement: now there was no-one.

'There!' The guard pointed up at the sky. I saw a small black smudge, travelling fast from outside the wall, pausing just over our heads, hovering, growing larger.

And the thought flashed into my mind: we must be hours overdue, back at the Colony. They'd be sending out search craft by now. I was bracing myself to rush forward and wave my arms about, get us airlifted out of there, when Pavel caught hold and pulled me back.

For a long moment the object hung there, spinning, above our heads. Then, with a rush, it fell to earth, embedding itself with a THUNK! in the dirt, round about where I would have been doing my impression of a windmill if Pavel hadn't stopped me.

No search craft. Just a medium-to-large-sized rock. Judging from the number of dents in the beaten earth, rocks falling from the sky was something that happened pretty often around here.

'No damage done,' the guard observed. 'Nice try, though. This way!' He was suddenly off again, following the line of the wall, till we came to a low doorway. We were right on his heels as he ducked inside, following in single file up the winding stair, round and round and round. My head was spinning when we came to a halt inside a small, square, watchtower.

'Just made it in time, I'd say.' The guard took a peek through one of the narrow slits in the outside wall. 'Yes! Come on!' He beckoned. 'Come and take a look! You'll like this.' He was looking at me as he said it, but I let Pavel and Sam go first. Out of the corner of my eye I'd caught a movement to my right. I swivelled my head a little; just enough to see that on the left it was the same. There were the people. Some of them. On either side, the top of the castle wall was crammed with men carrying bows and arrows, crouching low, heads down below the top of the stonework.

'Luke!' Pavel's voice. He beckoned me towards one of the narrow window slits, looking towards the landward side. I had a queasy feeling that I knew already what I was going to see.

'I think we have just caught up with Sam's Romans,' he said softly.

TEN

There were the Romans. Hundreds more than the bunch that had passed us earlier on. Dug in for a long siege, judging by the neat rows of tents, with campfires at regular intervals. Trenches and palisades zig-zagging towards the castle wall. The huge catapult thing that had been lobbing rocks over the wall. And, between their camp and the castle, three towers built out of tree trunks and branches, covered with dripping wet animal hides.

'Belfries,' I remembered aloud. The guard nodded.

Sam finally found his voice. 'What happens now?'

'Now—' I began, before I was drowned out by a fanfare of Roman trumpets, followed by the steady beat of kettledrums. With a cry of 'Long live the Emperor!' the three towers slowly started to move towards us on their solid wooden wheels. 'Well,' I said, 'you can see what they're doing now. They push the belfries forward until they reach the castle wall. Then they let down the front to form a drawbridge and storm in over the top. Then it's every man for himself. How are you at hand-to-hand fighting, Sam?'

Sam gave a strangled sob. 'Isn't someone going to *stop* them?'

Can't say I fancied my own chances much, if it came to one-to-one. There was nothing to stop the belfries coming all the way. No moat. No ditch. No outer ring of barricades. Not so much as a molehill. I glanced at the men crouching along the battlements, the look on their faces. Those belfries weren't going to even get close.

Wheels rumbling. Voices yelling. Drums drumming. Trumpets blaring. Sword hilts beating on shields. Warfare can seriously damage your hearing.

'What's going to happen to us?' moaned Sam. I pulled my face into a hideous leer and drew my forefinger across my throat.

'Dr Pavlov?' I don't know what he thought Pavel was going to do, except look up from his note taking and murmur, 'Stay calm.' Catching my eye. Looking from me to Sam and back; frowning slightly as he shook his head.

I draped my arm around Sam's shoulder. 'Only kidding,' I said soothingly. 'It'll be OK. You'll see.'

The way I saw it, if the guard, when he met us crawling up out of a hole in the ground, didn't think we were enemy spies sneaking in, that must mean that our side had had people down there. And for a very good reason.

The towers were picking up speed now, wobbling dangerously as they hit the downward slope and some of the men who'd been pushing leapt aboard and tried to elbow their way to the top, keen to be first over the wall. Rather them than me. The archers, still keeping out of sight, flexed the fingers of their right hands and nocked arrows to their bowstrings.

'Any minute now!' the guard murmured to himself. 'Wait for it! Stea-dy!'

Bingo! As he spoke, the belfry away out on our left seemed to falter, one wheel jammed fast in the earth. The trumpets quavered. And the voices. Battlecries turned to shrieks as, slowly, the whole thing keeled over, the trapped wheel sinking up to its hub, taking the other one on that side with it, while the wooden struts buckled, the weight of a log tore it free from the ropes that held it and bodies began to fall, legs treading air, willing themselves sideways, out of the way of tumbling tree trunks and sodden, smothering cow hides.

'Fire at will!'

And our archers leapt up and began pouring arrows into the tumbling tower and the bodies leaping from it. Some of the arrows were streaming fire. The water-soaked hides dangled bunched up and useless. Leaves, branches and timbers caught. Flames leapt up.

'Yess-s-s! Oh, well done, the miners!' cried the guard, clapping me so hard on the shoulder I staggered forward and bumped my head against the wall. 'Well done, lad!'

I smiled, modestly, and a bit dizzily. (No way you'd get me down there, burrowing like a mole under the path of that thing, but this wasn't the time to tell him.)

It was almost funny, the way the right-hand tower went. The undermining must have been spot-on, because the thin crust of earth just gave way all in one piece. The whole thing subsided, in slow motion, into the ground, leaving the men on the bottom storey floundering like non-swimmers, trying to keep their heads above the soil pouring in on them.

The middle tower was still trundling forward, but faltering. Like it was trying to smell out the third tunnel somewhere in its path. It never reached it. Men jumping down and pushers breaking away, running to help the wounded. Finally it stopped.

Our side went totally bananas. The archers were whooping and stomping. Shouting and making rude gestures at the Romans. Sam was leaping about and hulloo-ing right along with them, all his fears forgotten. Then one of the defenders flung out his arms and swallow-dived to the ground below. There was a sudden rush for cover.

We were under fire. Arrows and slingshot keeping our heads down, so the Roman stretcher teams could collect their wounded.

Safe in the little stone room, Sam was still doing his victory dance. 'Oh, wow! Oh, golly! Oh golly-gosh!' he crowed breathlessly. 'Did you see 'em, Luke? Did you see 'em?' Like we'd just won the Interplanetary Cup or something.

I felt sick. This was war; the kind that hasn't happened on earth for centuries, even in the drone-zones. People out there getting wasted. And for what? I sank down with my back against the wall, closed my eyes and let everything go black.

From far away I heard a voice: 'Must have caught a ricochet.'

There were people bending over me. I prised my eyes open. Slowly the craggy, reliable face of MainTech One swam into focus.

MainTech One? Was that likely? On balance, no. The world gave a lurch, and reality kicked in. It wasn't MainTech One; it was the guard. 'That looks nasty,' he opined.

Now it was Pavel bending over me: 'There is a doctor here?'

I pulled my leg back and struggled to sit upright. 'I don't want a doctor!' Not one from around here. I riffled through my memory banks. My leg. The cut on my leg. 'The stone that caveman threw at me,' I said. 'Remember?'

Pavel smiled reassuringly. 'I remember.' Seemed like it happened so long ago, I was half-wondering if I'd dreamed it.

'Let me see,' said Pavel.

I stuck out my leg again. 'It just needs cleaning up a bit,' I said.

Pavel peered at it, then nodded: 'I think you're right. Soap and water is all we need.' He straightened up and turned to the guard: 'You have somewhere we can wash?'

'Wash?' The guard scratched his head. 'You want a wash?'

'Just soap and clean water.'

'I'd like a bath, please,' said Sam.

'Soap? A bath?' I could see from the guard's face he was going to be really, really sorry to have to disappoint us. Then, to my total amazement, he said, 'You want a bath? Of course you do.' And he was off again, down the stairs, calling over his shoulder, 'This way!' I got to my feet and limped after him.

Sam pranced merrily along behind, beside, in front; pausing to wait while we caught up, then slipping behind again, so he could whisper in my ear, 'Don't look so worried!'

'Why shouldn't I be worried?'

'Haven't you worked it out yet?' He winked, hideously, one side of his face concertina-ing up, like Quasimodo.

'Worked what out?'

'What's going on! I have. I just gave him the final test that clinched it!'

'Tell me!'

'Later!' he chirruped. 'Tell you later!'

ELEVEN

Inside, and underground, the castle was like a three-dimensional maze. The guard led us upstairs and downstairs, through cavernous and empty rooms. Past ragged niches, like the diggers hacking them out of the rock lost heart before they were finished. As the guard bowled ahead, he flapped a hand to left or right, pointing out the dormitories, the armouries, the wine-store, the granary, the chapel, giving us the full guided tour, till Pavel reminded him that we were supposed to be on our way to a nice, hot bath, and we found ourselves plunging deeper underground. Cobwebs clustered, damp dripped from the ceiling and ran down the walls, and torches gave off more smoke than light. At the end of the deepest, darkest narrowest passage, our way was blocked by a solid oak door, with a brass plate engraved in wiggly gothic lettering:

DR D D DEE
Astrologer
Alchimiste
Apothecarie
Ingeniator
Fortunes tolden
Wartes cured
Maggottes for her, by ye daye or by ye weke.

'Fascinating!' murmured Pavel. 'Dr Dee. Of course!'

'Pavel!' I tugged at his sleeve. 'I told you I don't want a doctor.' For answer, he just pointed at the scrap of paper tacked underneath the main menu, with a message scrawled in pencil:

Haircut 3p
Bath (with soap) 2p

The guard knocked on the door.

A spyhole slid open and a bloodshot eye peered out. 'You can't come in right now. The doctor's busy.'

Pavel said, 'Please. We are not here for the doctor. Only for the baths.' The eye flickered up and down, not much liking what it saw, fixing at last on the guard. '*All* of you?'

'Just these three,' said the guard.

'Huh! No surprises there, then.' The eye looked the three of us over again. 'That'll be two pence each. IDs, please.'

I wondered what the company accountants would make of three two-penny withdrawals. That was their problem.

'OK. You can come in now.'

The door creaked slowly open.

I said, 'Wow!' I couldn't help myself. It was like – WOW!

It was your classic schlock-horror wizard's kitchen. The centrepiece was a seething cauldron over a huge open fire, flames leaping, sparks flying, smoke curling itself into unlikely shapes; fragments of light dancing and flashing and glowing in the darkest corners of the room. All along one wall there were shelves of tall glass jars filled with liquids and powders and crystals. Stacked up against another, tottering piles of thick, dusty books. I saw a brass orrery, with moons circling round the planets, and all the planets spinning round the sun. And a stuffed crocodile hanging from the ceiling, which turned its head and winked at me, I swear. A blackboard, covered in mystic calculations. Maps, diagrams, graphs and star charts, pinned on every spare bit of wall.

And the man himself? Dr D D Dee?

'Be with you in a minute!' came a cheery voice from behind the workbench on the far side of the room. Slowly, above a small sea of glass bottles and tubes that bubbled and steamed and fizzed and dripped, a pointy hat surfaced. Below it, a pair of eyes. 'I'm Dr Dee. Welcome to my humble abode. How may I help you?'

'Don't let us disturb your work,' said Pavel. 'We are here only for a wash and brush up.'

'Ah! Over there.' A disembodied hand rose up above the glassware, waving towards a low archway in the gloomiest corner of the room.

'After you, Sam,' I offered generously.

Sam was trying to form an orderly queue behind me. 'You're the one that most needs a bath,' he said.

'You said you wanted one. I didn't.'

Pavel shook his head and smiled and sighed: 'You two!' Whistling a little tune between his teeth, to show how nervous he wasn't, he stepped past the two of us, ducking his head through the low archway. Little wisps of smoke, or steam, crept out, as the door opened ahead of him. And closed behind him. After a few moments we heard him call out 'It's OK. Here is everything we need.'

Sam took two steps towards it, no more, before the door swung open again. Long tendrils of mist reached out, wrapping themselves around him and Sam was gathered in. Gone.

I edged forward. 'Pavel? Sam?' No answer. I looked around. At the guard and Dr D D Dee – what I could see of him, a slithering shape-shifter behind all those bottles and tubes. What would you do? Outnumbered two-to-one by the natives? I took a deep breath and plunged through, into the unknown.

And found myself in a fairly ordinary changing-room. Black-and-white tiled floor. A mosaic of dolphins leaping round the walls. A stone bench to sit on. And a pair of bathers, a bathrobe with matching slippers and a pile of fluffy towels. All in matching purple. Sam's favourite colour, I remembered. Certainly not mine, but what the heck. So I changed and, arming myself with sponge, soap and shampoo from a little wicker basket, headed through the door opposite, hearing Sam's voice again: 'Luke! Luke! Where are you? This way, Luke! Come and see!'

And found the two of them lolling in a stone-lined pool of warm, shallow water, about ten metres across, water spewing out of the mouths of bronze fishes perched on the corners. Life-size, painted statues in niches round the wall. Mosaics on the bottom of the pool, Neptune with his beard and crown and trident, plus half a dozen octopi and scores of little fishes.

'It's a Roman bath, Luke!' crowed Sam.

'A natural hot spring,' nodded Pavel.

A *Roman* bath?

'Well, what did you expect?' demanded Sam. 'A regular bathroom?'

I shook my head. I hadn't been expecting anything in particular. My mistake, maybe.

The water was so shallow, even scaredy-cat Sam felt free to fool around, walking his hands along and kicking with his legs, pretending to be swimming. I sat on the edge, while Pavel soaped and bathed the cut on my leg. It still stung a fair bit as I slid down into the water. But it got better.

I was waiting for Sam to share his big idea with us. About the how and why of us being here. Now that it was just the three of us together, what was to stop him? If he really thought he knew. From the glances he kept sneaking my way, I guessed he was bursting for me to ask.

I wasn't going to rush him. I could wait. I leaned back and closed my eyes.

If Sam could work it out, then I could. Sam didn't know anything I didn't. The trouble was, things had happened so fast since we left the Colony that morning, I hadn't had time to *think*. First the Blue Mountain and Open Sesame and Shangri-la. Then Romans and cavemen, quite apart from having to avoid being half-frozen to death. Escaping down a coalmine . . . then up a mineshaft . . . Pieces of a jigsaw. Back in the Colony I'd had too few; now suddenly there were way too many. The only thing I was sure of was that they were all part of the same picture. If I could just stand back a minute, take a proper look . . .

And now here we were in what seemed to be a medieval castle under siege. Things could be worse. Castles I knew about. Castles I could handle.

I must have dozed for a bit. When I opened my eyes, I was alone. I waited for a moment, just to check that it hadn't all been a dream and I wasn't lying in my own little bed at home. No such luck. So I hauled myself out and grabbed the last dry towel. Found my own clothes, not in a heap on the floor where I'd left them, but in a neat pile on the bench, sponged clean and ironed, as good as new. Which was nice.

Back in the wizard's kitchen, Pavel was prowling up and down the storage shelves playing a game he'd just invented. Name This Chemical! None of the jars had labels on, so it was look, shake, off with the lid, rub a pinch between your fingers, smell, and – sometimes (don't try this at home, kids) – taste. 'Sodium!' I heard him mutter, jotting it down in his notebook.

He picked up the next one and considered it. Shook it gently. 'Potassium chlorate, I think.' He unstoppered the lid, sniffed once, twice, and nodded to me: 'Potassium chlorate. I thought so. That could be useful.'

'For what?' I asked.

He put a finger to his lips and winked at me. Then he carefully put the lid back, replaced the jar and made a jotting in his notebook. 'But this one beside it . . .' He paused, frowning, over a jar of greyish, brownish matter. 'I don't know. Do you?'

I shrugged.

He shook it about. Tipped it upside down and back again. At last he shook his head. 'I've really no idea.'

He flashed me an odd look as he took off the lid and sniffed at the contents. Offered it to me. I took a sniff. Nothing.

'You can't win 'em all,' I said.

'No?' He gave me that slow, knowing smile of his and reached for another jar. In the assorted glassware on the workbench the liquid was still happily fizzing and popping and bubbling without any help from Dr Dee, who was squatting on the floor on the far side of the room, with the guard and Sam, fooling around with some kind of wooden toy.

They'd set the pointy hat up as a target and were firing small, round pebbles at it, from a thing that looked a bit like a tiny seesaw. From one end – nearest the target – dangled a little bucket of sand. The other was carved out like a spoon, with a pebble resting in it. Load up, let go, down goes the sand, up and over goes the pebble, and – *thunk!* – down goes the pointy hat. Almost.

Sam sorted through a little heap of pebbles on the floor beside him, picked one out and handed it to the doctor, saying, 'Now try this one. Don't forget to weigh it first.' The doctor weighed it carefully on a hand-held set of scales, made a note, then passed the pebble to the guard so he could load up again.

Then Sam looked up and saw me. 'Hi, Luke! Come and see! I'm going to show them how to build a trebuchet. Much better than that old catapult the Romans are using, yeah?'

'Yeah.'

'I don't know why no-one here's thought of it before. You see, by varying the weight-to-counterweight ratio (that's the size of the rock and the amount of sand in the bucket), we can have precision bombing. If we use a smaller rock, that should give us a flatter flight path. And a longer range, if you'd like to move the target back a bit,' he said to the doctor, 'so I can show Luke what I mean.'

The doctor crawled forward and started shifting his

battered headgear along the floor.

'A bit further back!' said Sam. 'No, not that far. That's good.' He nodded to the guard. 'OK, fire away!'

'Have a care!' yelled the guard, letting fly at the same time.

The doctor flung himself out of the way. The pebble shot through the air and made another dent in the hat. Sam moseyed over and peered at it. 'Hm! Could do with a bit more power behind it. If we could get rid of that spoon shape – replace it with a sling. That would give us more power, more range. More maths to work out, too, of course. But I don't mind, if you don't.'

'Building it full size! Phew!' The doctor frowned and shook his head. 'It's going to take an awful lot of wood.'

'The wood's no problem,' said Sam. 'I know where we can get the wood. It's finding enough rocks the same size and weight, so I can do the necessary practice runs. That rock the Romans fired at us earlier on would be about right for starters. What happened to it?'

'I'll ask, shall I?' said the guard, scrambling to his feet.

I said, 'Sorry to spoil the party. But is there anything to eat around here? I'm starving!' If I'd wanted to stop the project in its tracks, I couldn't have chosen a better way to do it.

'Starving?' exclaimed the doctor, throwing his hands in the air.

'We can't have that!' cried the guard.

'What shall we do?'

'Feed them, of course!'

'Double-quick.'

'Spit-spot.'

'Chop-chop!'

TWELVE

Moments later the three of us, plus our guide-stroke-guard, were back in the courtyard sitting under a lopsided awning, round a table with a red checked cloth and a candle stuck in a wax-encrusted bottle, under a sign on the wall that said, *Ye doe not hav to be madde to worken heere, but it doth helpe*. Out of the shadows an aged crone, wrapped in a shapeless bundle of rags, came shuffling towards us. Her face was wizened, mottled pink and yellow-beige, like a dried-out apple.

'Dinner for four, please, Aged Crone!' the guard sang out before she was halfway. She stopped, teetered, turned and hobbled back into the gloom. When she showed again, she was carrying four bowls on a tray. She slopped them down on the table.

'Loverly-jubberly!' murmured the guard. He picked his bowl up in both hands and started slurping straight from it, while the three of us waited politely for the crone to finish buffing up our greasy spoons on her even greasier shawl.

I stared down at the stuff in my bowl. It looked horribly like that curry our autocook kept serving up when it was on the blink.

I took a good sniff. It didn't smell like curry. It didn't smell of anything, much. Sam wrinkled his nose: 'What's in it?'

'A little bit of everything,' nodded the crone. She

reached out a finger and thumb and playfully pinched his cheek. 'Everything that's needed for a growing boy.'

Pavel took a spoonful. Then another.

The crone went on nodding. She seemed to find it hard to stop, as if her head was joined on by a spring.

Sam pulled a face and pushed his bowl to one side. Still nodding, the crone hobbled huffily away into the gloom.

'Try it!' said Pavel. 'It's OK.'

So I did. It was OK. I s'pose. Better than nothing. Just. Not nice, or nasty. But I could feel my stomach slowly filling up in a very comforting way.

The guard belched, wiped his mouth across his sleeve and stood up. 'Time I was off!' he said. 'I expect you three'd like a bit of time alone, to talk things over.' He bowled away, little legs scissoring, feet just skimming the ground.

All around the courtyard, life was getting under way again. Soldiers practising sword fights. Archers archering. Little kids running around, playing War, shrieking and hollering. Women gossiping or singing as they cooked the evening meal, sewed, rocked the baby, whatever. All of it echoing and re-echoing off the walls. So we were able to talk things over, with no fear of being overheard. So I said to Pavel (ignoring Sam), 'What do *you* think's going on here?'

Pavel, blowing gently on a spoonful of stew, shook his head: 'I'm not sure yet.'

I said, 'Sam's sure. Sam thinks he's worked it out already. Don't you, Sam?'

Sam, looking very pleased with himself said, 'It's simple! Isn't it?'

I glanced at Pavel. Then answered for the both of us, 'No.'

Sam said, 'It's got to be the Company.'

My spoon stopped, poised in mid-air, halfway to my mouth. 'The Company?' I said.

That was It? The Answer To It All?

Pavel went on sipping at his stew, without looking up. 'You think the Company is behind all this?'

'It's got to be!' Sam said again. 'The Company owns the whole planet. Nothing happens on Omega Seven that the Company doesn't know about, right? This place is huge! How could it be here without the Company knowing about it? So it has to be the Company!'

He'd flipped. Totally. I put down my spoon. 'Sam,' I said firmly. 'Take a look around you. Does this look like a Company operation to you? It's a muddle. A mess! The uniforms aren't uniform. There's dust and slime and cobwebs everywhere. The buildings look like they were thrown together by an earthquake. The food's hardly fit to chuck down the waste disposal.'

'A-ha!' said Sam. Don't you just hate it when people say a-ha like that? 'A-ha! That's all put in on purpose to confuse us.'

I glanced at Pavel. Pavel had given up on his stew and was sitting quietly listening, polishing his glasses.

I said, 'OK, Sam. I'm confused. What about the Blue Mountain? How come we just walked through from there to here?'

Sam smiled, annoyingly: 'That's the easiest thing of all to explain. We never *got* to the Blue Mountain. We only *thought* we did. It was just some kind of hologram.'

'*Just* a hologram? It's about a kilometre high!'

Sam carried on regardless: 'That's why it was so easy to walk through to where we are now. We were *meant* to walk through. Because we've been *chosen*.'

'Chosen for what?'

Sam said cautiously: 'I'm just guessing here. But I think this is some kind of experiment. I think we're being tested in some way.'

'Tested! For what?'

Sam shook his head: 'I don't know. Maybe we're not supposed to know. But don't you get the feeling we're being watched?'

'No.' I flapped my hand towards the castle wall: 'All those people getting hurt out there? Killed even? That was just part of some experiment?'

Sam shook his head: 'I don't think anyone really got hurt.'

'Huh? I saw blood. Broken bones. Men on fire, leaping from about ten metres up. Logs falling on top of them. What were they, then? Stuntmen? Computer simulations? More holograms? Anyway, *I* got hurt!' I stuck my leg up on the table, my foot right under his nose, which made him jerk back a bit. He had to admit that was real.

'You were only hurt a little bit,' he said sulkily. 'I don't think that was meant to happen.'

'If that rock that came flying over the wall a while ago had flattened us, I don't s'pose that would have been meant to happen either, but they'd still have been scraping what was left of us off the floor.'

'But it didn't, did it?' he cried triumphantly. 'You see!

Nothing's going to hurt us while we're here.'

'Oh, no?'

'Look, if the Company's set up this whole thing . . .'

'That's a big IF,' I said.

He glared at me. 'I said, if the Company's doing this, it has to be for a very good reason. We don't have to know what the reason is. All we have to do is co-operate. Do our best.'

'Helping them build a trebuchet. So they can kill more Romans. You think that's what the Company wants you to do?'

'If it's not, they'll stop me, right?' He suddenly reached out and grabbed my hand. 'Stay calm, Luke. Trust the Company. The Company's taking care of us. Haven't you noticed, whenever we really need something, it's there? A place to shelter. A way out. Even a bath!'

'Praise the Company. Hallelujah!' I twisted my hand away and wiped it on my shirt.

'They even had my favourite colour bathers!'

'A fluke,' I said. And before I could add that anyway, purple just happened to be *my least* favourite, so where did that leave us . . .

'Wasn't,' he snapped.

I tried another tack. 'Anything we need, you said? Right now, what I really need is some pudding.' I called into the shadows,' Excuse me! Um. Aged crone?'

The crone's face swam into focus. 'You want seconds?'

'We'd like some pudding, please.' As she shuffled towards us, I turned to Sam again: 'I think I'll have the chocolate and nut ice cream sundae with mocha sauce. How about you, Sam?'

The crone, cackling mirthlessly, lifted up her bucket

crusted with dry stew and topped up the bowls with the same gunge as before.

'Sorry, Sam,' I said. 'No pudding.'

'You'll see,' he pouted. 'We'll get out of this. Just trust the Company.'

'Oh, good!' I said. 'So there's nothing at all to worry about.'

He glared at me. 'This food's disgusting. I'm going to find an autocook. So there!'

He sauntered away, narrowly missing being kebabed ear-to-ear by a practising archer.

'Let him go,' Pavel said quietly.

'He's wrong though, isn't he? I know he's wrong. I know it's not the Company.'

Pavel toyed with the stuff in his bowl, lumps coloured pink and orange and creamy-white struggling to the surface before going down for the third time. 'I think, Luke, you should still consider carefully what he has said.'

What was to consider? Sam said we'd been hand-picked for some Company experimental project. I knew the Company couldn't be behind it.

The old woman was still hovering.

Pavel said sociably, 'This stew is exceedingly good. With bacon, cured the old-fashioned way, if I am not mistaken. Always in my grandmother's kitchen there was a big pot of preserving salts, with the bacon left to cure. Is that the way you do it? May I see?' He pointed towards the smoky depths, reaching with his other hand for his notebook and pencil. The crone, nodding, beaming between toothless gums, turned to lead the way.

When Pavel came back, sliding into the seat opposite, 'Well?' I said. 'What was all that about?'

'Most interesting!' he murmured. 'The methods these people use for preserving food are exactly the same as those that used to be on Earth.' He began quietly studying the notes he'd taken, underlining, circling, arrowing.

I said, 'You heard about what happened to Mr Strangeways?'

He nodded.

'It's happening to us, isn't it?'

He looked up at me and smiled. 'Maybe. But there are three of us. We'll be OK if we stick together.'

I said, 'You're enjoying this, aren't you?'

Calmly he nodded: 'It's a puzzle. I like puzzles.'

I leaned across the table towards him. 'We've got to get out of here!' I whispered.

Pavel shook his head: 'I think there is no hurry.'

'We've got to warn the Colony about this place, while we still can. Before we end up like Mr Strangeways, with our brains so scrambled we can't make any sense of what we've seen.'

He folded up his notebook and slipped it in his pocket. 'Not yet, I think.'

'Tonight? As soon as it's dark? I've been thinking. All we need is a rope and some kind of a diversion.'

'I think we should hang around a little longer.' He stood up. 'There are one or two things I want to check out,' he announced. 'Sam's happy enough. We'll let him go on thinking this is a Company operation.'

'What about me?'

He bent his head towards me and said softly, 'What you can do, Luke, is do a little snooping for me. Talk to people. I can't ask too many questions, but no-one gets suspicious when a kid asks questions. Between us, we will solve this mystery. That is what we have to do now, yes?'

I gave him a doubtful look.

'And no more fighting with Sam, huh? We should be a team. Solidarity, yes?'

'I s'pose. If you say so.'

'Now!' he said thoughtfully. 'I wonder if there is a blacksmith round here? Or an armourer. An armourer would do.'

Maybe the crone had some old saucepan with a hole in it that needed fixing. And this was Pavel's good deed for the day. I didn't ask. He wandered off.

THIRTEEN

And then there was one. Just me, sitting alone with the remains of four bowls of iffy stew. I sat staring out across the courtyard, while the shadows lengthened and the sky clouded over. The women began gathering in the washing and the kids. The men played at cards or darts or dice, drank a mug of ale, or wandered about in little groups. They didn't look so different from people in the Colony. There were even faces, here and there, that I half-recognised. I guess there are only so many variations you can work on two eyes, two ears, one nose, one mouth. I was starting to feel quite at home. Which was why it made good sense not to hang around.

I'd made up my mind what I was going to do.

The Truth was Out There somewhere. Maybe Pavel would find it. Maybe not. Meanwhile, someone had to try and make it back to the Colony. Tell them. Warn them. Security could take it from there.

Escape. That's what I had to do. As soon as it was properly dark. Down the mineshaft, and back through the tunnel system. I'd need something better than a smouldering branch to light the way this time. I checked out the wax-encrusted bottles on the red-checked tables, wondering how many candles I could take without the old woman missing them.

It was like Pavel always said: look around you; think sideways; improvise. I might even get lucky and find a passageway that came out the other side of the Blue Mountain. A piece of chalk, so I could mark the way I'd come, make it easy to back-track, take a different turning . . . Wasn't there a blackboard and chalk in Dr Dee's lab? I'd just mosey on down and tell him I was looking for Sam. Sidle over . . .

But what would I do if Sam was there? Would I tell him I was getting out? Give him a chance to come with me?

No way! Chances were he'd ruin everything.

I went on sitting. It was still too light to be doing anything about my break for freedom yet. So I just sat, enjoying the evening light, watching the people. Noticed a woman leaning over the low stone wall of the mineshaft, peering down. Couldn't keep from staring, she looked so much like Ma. Except I couldn't really imagine Ma dressed in ankle-length homespun, fetching water from the well, swinging the brimming bucket up on to her head without spilling a drop.

Hang on a minute! *What* well? What happened to the mineshaft?

I got up and sauntered over, hands shaking inside my pockets, trying hard to look casual. Picked up a stone and tossed it over the edge. Counted, One, Two! – no more – before I heard the splash.

They'd flooded the mine. To stop the Romans burrowing in. Or us getting out. Which would mean someone knew we didn't really belong. Like Sam said, someone watching us. I shivered.

Look on the bright side. If I had made it back alone, without the other two to tell the same story, would anyone have believed me anyway?

I hoped the little kid with the candle in his hat had made it out OK.

There had to be a way out. Let's think of this as a VR game, I told myself. I'd played enough of them in my time. VR was supposed to prepare you for the hard knocks of real life. There was always a way out, if you thought about it hard enough. I decided I might as well do as Pavel said. Start asking some questions. So I went back and gathered up the bowls and spoons and carried them through into the gloom, where the crone sat knitting beside a huge, bubbling cauldron.

'That was really nice!' I lied. 'Phew! Yeah!' I rubbed my stomach. 'I feel really full!'

She seemed pleased. Took the leftovers from me, one bowl at a time, and scraped them back into the pot. 'Want not, waste not,' she said.

I groped around for something else to say. 'Er. What's that you're knitting?'

She held it up: 'Comforts for our brave soldiers.' It was another one of those loose-knit grey shirts like the guard was wearing.

'Very nice,' I said. It was horrible. I tried not to sound too keen, in case she offered to make one for me. 'My name's Luke.'

She went on knitting.

I ploughed on: 'So, what's your name, then?'

No answer.

'I can't just call you Aged Crone.'

'You can call me it, if you want.' Her mouth split into a toothless smile. 'It's what I am. I've got warts and everything,' she added proudly.

'OK, then, er, Aged Crone. So, what is this place

exactly?' I flapped a hand towards the courtyard. 'I mean . . . All This.'

'All this?' she nodded. All this? This is a Castle, Luke.'

'I *know* it's a castle!' I took a deep breath and fixed the look of innocent childish curiosity back in place. 'What castle, exactly? Has it got a name?'

'A-ha! That's for me to know and you to find out.' She waved a waggish finger, dropped two more stitches and knitted on regardless.

'If this is just *a* castle, not *the* castle, then there must be others.' (Though the idea of Omega Seven being littered with undiscovered castles . . .)

'Must there?' she pondered. 'I suppose there must be, if you say so. Make up the fire for me, will you, Luke.' Pointing to a heap of wood in the corner.

'OK.' I pushed a couple of middle-sized logs in among the glowing embers in the grate, then, thinking the odd joke might loosen her tongue a bit, I said: 'How does a fire feel when it's just been made up?'

She shook her head. 'I don't know. How does a fire feel when it's just been made up?'

'Grate-full! Yes?'

'Grateful?' Slowly her head began to nod. 'Grateful. Yes. I suppose it would be.'

If at first you don't succeed . . .

I pointed to the pot of stew simmering away: 'Do you know what ghosts eat for lunch?' Pause. 'Ghoul-ash!'

'Goulash!' she nodded. 'I didn't know that. That's interesting.'

Third time lucky?

'And do you know what they eat for dinner?'

'Who? Ghosts?'

I nodded. 'Spook-etti!'

'Spaghetti!' she said sadly. Tears started oozing from her eyes. 'I haven't seen spaghetti since before the war.' She fished out a scrap of grubby rag, wiped her eyes, blew her nose, then absent-mindedly threw the rag into the cauldron and stirred it in. 'Want not, waste not.'

Maybe I should have made a connection then with something I'd discovered earlier in the Colony, but I was too tired to think properly. I gave up. Outside, the sun had set and stars were doing their thing all over the darkening sky. I knew I ought to check up on Sam; make sure he was OK. Solidarity and that, like Pavel said. But it had been a long day. And not a half-decent meal to be had anywhere along the way. So I slipped back indoors and curled up by the Aged Crone's cooking-fire to sleep.

FOURTEEN

The first thing I saw next morning when I looked out of the door was a huge heap of wood, from whole tree trunks down to little twiggy bits with crumpled leaves still hanging off. I'd underestimated Sam. When Sam said, 'The wood's no problem. I know where we can get the wood,' I never would have thought he'd have the chutzpah. The difference between us was that Sam knew, wherever he went – even down a narrow, crumbling tunnel in the dark, to the very edge of the enemy camp – the Company was looking after him. I wouldn't have put it past him to go strolling up to the nearest sentry and ask permission. '*That pile of wood you've got there . . . I don't s'pose you'll be using it again, will you? So you won't mind if we . . . ?*'

I thought the whole tunnel system had been flooded. Sam knew better.

I sprinted up to the battlements, took careful cover behind a merlon and peered cautiously round. Between the castle and the Roman camp, where the three belfries had been, there were now two heaps of ashes and, in between, nothing but a sprinkling of dead leaves and four wooden wheels. The wheels must have been too big to go through. I guessed we didn't need the wheels anyway. Then Sam himself came bouncing up the stairs towards me.

'Sam—' I began.

'Hold that!' he said, thrusting one end of a tape measure into my hand.

'What's this?'

'Just hold it straight.'

'Sam, I really don't think you ought to take chan—'

He was trotting away towards the other end of the allure, paying out the tape.

'Sam! Look, all I'm saying is, we don't know for sure it's the Co—'

Sam's voice floated back, 'Can you believe no-one here actually knows the exact length of this wall?'

'So what?' I yelled. 'It's a wall. So long as it reaches from one end to the other—'

'Sorry! Can't hear you!' He just kept on going till he reached the other corner tower. Waved to me to let go and swiftly rolled up the tape. Took out some kind of wood-and-brass thing, laid it flat on the end merlon and rested his chin on the stone beside it.

'Sam! What are you doing? Get down you drone!' I kept myself bent double as I ran towards him. Sam made another note, then strolled along to meet me, head bobbing past the embrasures like a duck in a fairground target-shoot.

'What are you doing?' I demanded.

'Calculating the exact position of that catapult. We don't want to build our trebuchet right in the line of fire, do we?'

'I guess not.'

He trotted off down the stairs again, 'Catch you later then!'

'If the Romans don't take your head off first!' I murmured under my breath.

Down in the bailey there was a team of men-at-arms sorting out the lengths of wood, Sam measuring and marking up, then setting them to work with saws and axes. Dr Dee, in his wizard's cloak, was fluttering here, there and everywhere, like a great, black, star-spangled bird, but anyone could see this was Sam's party.

Still keeping my head well down till I was sure of being out of the line of fire, I moved off along the side wall. Just checking. Making sure there wasn't some blindingly obvious way of escape. A postern gate or tradesmen's entrance. A stairway, even, leading down the outside of the wall. Not that I expected it to be that easy. And I was right. There was nothing. The castle was built on a spit of land that jutted out over a river canyon. The walls rose straight up from the cliff, so it was hard to see where the rock ended and the masonry began. The landward side was blockaded by the Roman army. Which left the approach to the main gate, a narrow bridge across the canyon, the last few metres a drawbridge, which was up. Even if it had been down, and the gate standing open, I'd have had more than second thoughts about trying to bluff my way through the posse of Romans guarding the far end. Looked like the same, mean bunch we saw when we first arrived.

I caught sight of Pavel once or twice, mingling. Fetching beer in stone bottles for the men working on the trebuchet, then taking back the empties. He'd got himself one of the crone's hand-knitted shirts so as to blend better, but he was still the only one wearing glasses.

I completed my tour of the battlements, then sloped back to the Aged Crone's to wash a few dishes, sweep the floors, and smear the grease over the tables so it was evenly spread before the first customers arrived. I filled her a couple of buckets from the well and checked out the water level while I was at it. No change.

'You're a good boy,' the crone nodded, smiling toothlessly. 'Looking after a poor, aged crone.'

I was looking after me. If the Romans did find a way in, I reckoned they'd still need someone with all their limbs to fetch and carry, do the washing up for them and so on. The kitchen seemed like the safest place to be.

After that I went around talking to people, like Pavel had told me to do. Got nowhere.

Everyone was really nice. The archers gave me a few lessons in archery. Told me a longbow could fire twelve shots a minute. Interesting, but not the sort of thing I needed to know, just at present. Crossbows? They didn't hold with crossbows, longer range, but no skill needed, any fool could fire a crossbow, nasty, sneaky, foreign things. And you'd be lucky to get two rounds a minute out of them. Noticed Pavel as I left, making himself useful, bringing up a fresh supply of arrows.

I cornered Dr Dee and asked the question that had been bugging me since I first read the brass plate on his door. 'Maggots for hire. Why would anyone want to hire maggots?'

He said, 'For cleaning out infected wounds, of course. To eat away the dead flesh, so new, healthy tissue can grow. There's many a soldier would have lost an arm or a leg – or his life! – if it wasn't for the humble maggot.'

Wished I hadn't bothered with that one.

Still I went on gathering information. The armourers wouldn't let me get away till I could recite the names of every piece of body armour off by heart. But as soon as I started in with the stuff that really mattered – Where did they come from? Who was in charge? Why were we here? And what's it all about? – they didn't want to know. Told me to push off (or words to that effect). Finally I ran out of people to talk to, so I just sat, soaking up the sun. Look on the bright side: there was no-one around to ask me why I couldn't find something more useful to do. No Tough-and-manly or Sweet-as-sugar hassling me with study programmes and fitness schedules and Is-anything-the-matter-Luke? Anything you want to talk about? Life in the Colony seemed like a million light years away, or something I'd once dreamed about.

What proof had I got that it hadn't all been a dream? Well, Ma and Pa, for a start. I missed them. In a way. I knew they must be missing me by now. It was OK for Pavel and Sam; there was no-one to worry about them, where they were, what they were up to.

Maybe this was the time to try out my new-found telepathic talents – if I had any. Security might not be able to get a trace on our IDs. But telepathy works on a different level, mind-direct-to-mind. Deep-space, you're talking years for a light-speed message to travel the distance. Telepaths, they could be in the same room. So I leaned back and closed my eyes Tried to empty my mind, the way Pa said you were supposed to do. Not as easy as you'd think.

What message to send? That was the question. *Hi, Ma and Pa. Sorry we got a bit held up, but don't worry about me, OK?* didn't quite fit the bill. Maybe a picture of this place – which wouldn't tell them much, unless I could key in images of everything that had happened, not just here, but back in the Colony. Start again. Clear my mind. Focus on our autocook that kept serving up curry . . . then Mr Strangeways disappearing . . . a football turned inside out . . . and the Blue Mountain.

The more pictures my brain conjured up, the harder I found it to keep them in their proper order. They kept changing places, regrouping, like a kaleidoscope, circles within circles, moving in a stately dance and, at the centre, a still, small point, which was the key. Maybe I was coming at it the wrong way. Maybe it wasn't the things themselves I should be looking at. Leave aside the stuff from back in the Colony and take a good, hard look at what had happened to us here. Not what, but why. *Why* Romans? *Why* a coalmine? *Why* a castle? What was the common thread?

'It's nice here, isn't it?' said Sam, parking himself down beside me.

'Huh?' The kaleidoscope shattered, pieces flying apart. Who was I kidding anyway? I was no telepath. Shangri-la and the castle were just a couple of lucky guesses, that was all. It was Sam who first started blethering on about Romans, and no way was I going to believe Sam was the teeniest bit psychic. And cavemen. Who was it who first mentioned cavemen?

Sam sighed happily, 'I haven't had so much fun since I left home.'

'Home?' I said sourly. 'Where is it you deeks call home, anyway?'

He looked surprised. 'Earth, of course. Eastern Zone, South Central. Wish my brothers could see this place!'

I sat up. 'Your brothers!'

'Yes. Two of them. And a sister.

'You mean, like, a real family? Ma and Pa, too?'

'Of course I've got a real family. What did you think?'

What did I think? Only what I'd heard. Word is . . .

'That I was hatched in a Company test tube or something?'

'Course not,' I lied.

Silence, then, 'I was head-hunted by the Company scouts when I was six years old.'

'I didn't know that.'

'How would you? Your parents are both Alphas, or you wouldn't be here.'

'What are yours then? They're not— ?'

'No, they're not Drones. They're Workers. Serves me right for showing off my party tricks,' he said bitterly. 'If I'd been *really* smart, I'd have played dumb.'

'Yeah.' I didn't know what else to say. So I went to fetch myself some lunch.

As I strolled back to my place in the sun, the trebuchet team, with much grunting and heave-ho-ing, began levering and winching the sections upright. The machine towered over everything in sight, bar the actual castle walls.

'It's looking good,' I said.

Sam stared at my bowl of stew. 'Do you actually like that stuff?' he asked.

'Like it?' I echoed. What kind of a dumb question was that?

Sam said, 'Why don't you use the autocook?'

'What autocook?'

'The one downstairs.'

'Huh?'

'Come on; I'll show you.'

Like an idiot, I put down my bowl and followed him. I was that desperate for a taste of real fast-food.

Down the winding stair we went. Along a passageway. Across a vast, dusty room. Then down another corridor. All the time was this nagging feeling that Sam was winding me up. There was no autocook. How could there be?

'Nearly there!' Sam chirruped. 'Just round the next corner and here it . . .' His voice tailed off into silence.

'Here it *isn't*,' I said, between gritted teeth. 'Nice one, Sam! Ha, ha! You really had me going there.'

I had to hand it to him; he did seem totally mystified. 'I don't understand,' he burbled. 'It *was* here. Right *here*!'

I tried not to show how disappointed I was. I shrugged my shoulders: 'Yeah, yeah, yeah! Now if you'll excuse me, I've got to be getting back. Things to do. People to see. Busy, busy, busy!' I stomped off, breaking in to a run once I turned the first corner, putting as big a distance between Sam and me as fast as I could.

I lied. I'd run out of people to talk to and ways of asking the same questions hours ago. So I started exploring the insides of the castle from top to bottom and end to end, looking for clues . . . a way out . . . anything. I *had* to get out! But there was *no way*. Felt more and more like one of Pavel's lab specimens, banging my head against an invisible wall. When I came out into the courtyard again, the trebuchet was up and loaded. A voice yelled, 'Have a care!'

The courtyard cleared in about two seconds flat, faces watching from the shadows. Someone tugged on a rope. The weighted arm dropped. The sling swung up and over. The stone flew from it, almost dead level, chipping sparks from the top of the wall. Sam was up on the ramparts again, getting a fix on the spot where the rock had landed, scribbling new calculations.

About twenty minutes later, what looked like the identical rock came sailing back. They dug it up, shovelled some earth from the counterweight bucket, loaded up and fired. The rock went higher this time, but not so far. 'Hey!' said Sam. 'Did you weigh that earth you just threw out? Well, weigh it *now*!'

By late afternoon, the castle had settled into a new routine. Not so much a battle; more like a demonstration of what the trebuchet versus the catapult could do.

Sam was in deek heaven. Every time that stone was fired by our side, Sam was up on the battlements to see it land and take new measurements, enemy arrows and slingshot whistling past his ears, safe inside an invisible ring of trust in the Company. And you know what? I'll swear I saw some of those missiles actually curve round him.

'Have you managed to find out anything?' asked Pavel, sliding into a seat at the dinner table beside me.

I shook my head: 'Nothing. Except these people have got to be from Earth, right? Because a life-form evolving on another planet to look exactly like humans, with medieval technology – and speaking modern English! – is about as likely as the one about the infinite number of monkeys with an infinite number of keyboards coming up with the complete works of . . . of . . . who was that guy who wrote all the plays?'

'Shakespeare?'

'Probably. So. Anyway. Maybe there's a bunch of earlier colonists the Company didn't know about. Simple-lifers.

Squatters from a hundred years back. So some of them would know about stealth devices, which is why none of the surveys picked them up. And hacking into computer systems. Maybe they've even got some way of slipping into and out of the Colony, through those underground tunnels we found, which would explain about things and even people going missing. And, and, and—' I was really on a roll now. 'And maybe two groups of them fell out, which is why there's our side and the Romans. The important thing is, is the Colony in danger? How much damage can these people do?'

Pavel said quietly, 'Or how much damage can the Colony do to them?'

'Oh! Right! So you think maybe all they're doing is sort of messing things up a bit, hoping we'll go away and leave them alone!' I wished! 'But that's not it, is it?' I finished lamely.

Pavel shook his head: 'I don't think so. Keep working at it.' He tucked his notebook away.

'So what's your theory?'

He smiled that slow smile of his. 'You wouldn't believe me if I told you.'

'Try me!'

'I think this is something we each have to work out for ourselves.'

'Why?'

He grinned. 'When you know the answer, you will understand why.'

'Just a hint, Pavel? Please.'

'OK.' He laughed and tapped the side of his nose. 'Use your nose, Luke! Use your nose!' Still chuckling to himself, he turned and walked away.

Use my nose? I sniffed the air. I couldn't smell anything. Nothing at all. Which should have told me something. But it didn't.

I couldn't see what he'd got to look so cheerful about. As if things weren't bad enough with Sam going native, now I'd got Pavel turning all mysterious on me.

FIFTEEN

I was dreaming again, that same kaleidoscope of autocooks and chessboards and footballs disappearing and reappearing and Romans in the gloaming and Mr Strangeways muttering over and over, 'I don't *understand*!' Pictures dancing in my head, forming a pattern, the answer to it all on the tip of my tongue – no, you don't see with your tongue. But it was almost like that. Like hearing a picture, feeling a sound . . .

I prised one eye open and saw the crone sitting rocking by the fire, nursing a leg of half-cured ham on her knee. 'I don't understand,' she said again. 'It doesn't make sense. Does it make any sort of sense to you?' she demanded. 'Stealing a jar of preserving salt and leaving a perfectly good leg of meat that was in it behind?'

I shook my head.

'And it's not just me that's been robbed either,' she nodded. 'Oh, no!' She gave me an odd, sort of sideways look, like I should know more about it than she did. 'There's the armourers,' she nodded. '*And* Dr Dee. Oh well. Want not, waste not, eh?' She tossed the ham into the stew-pot, where it sank without trace. And picked up her knitting again. 'Help yourself to breakfast.'

But I wasn't hungry. My stomach felt like it was tying itself into a rock-hard knot.

Outside, the bailey felt different somehow. Quiet. Too quiet. The only signs of movement coming from around the armourers' workshop. The Security guard – the one who'd checked us in when we first arrived – was standing in the middle of them with a notebook in one hand, a pencil in the other. 'One bag of – charcoal,' he read aloud, ' – standard. And when was this bag of charcoal brought up from the store?'

The armourers all started answering at once.

'Yesterday night!'

'About seven o'clock.'

'Eight! Nearer eight.'

'Call it seven-thirty, yeah!'

'Yeah.'

'We left it there—'

'Right there!'

'—ready for this morning.'

'*And* someone's taken a wheel off the barrow!'

'Let's have that one at a time, please!' The guard licked his pencil again. 'Forget about the barrow for the moment. One bag – charcoal. Yes-ter-day night. About – what time?' He suddenly spun round to face me. 'Sorry, Luke, can't stop. I've got to interview the doctor next. Matter of one jar of sulphur, three-quarters full. Sulphur, saltpetre and charcoal!' he chortled. 'What does that suggest to you, Luke? Hey? Hey?'

Like this was something to do with me? I said weakly, 'Maybe they'll turn up, if you just wait. Things do, don't they?' Getting this feeling of déjà-vu. Edging away, thinking, How wrong can you be? I'd thought the people here were somehow behind the strange disappearances from the Colony. But now it was happening to them too. Things disappearing, without rhyme or reason. The three of us marked down for the fall-guys, I could see it in the guard's eyes. And the crone's, too. This was more than I could handle on my own. I said, 'Do you know where I can find Dr Pavlov?'

The guard said, 'Who?'

I looked all over for Pavel. Couldn't find him anywhere. Thought I'd lost Sam, too, then spotted him perched cross-legged on top of the battlements, like a pixie on a mushroom, surveying the enemy camp.

I called out to him – 'Sam!' – as I came up the last few steps.

'Hi, Luke.' He didn't even bother to look round. 'Come and see. This is getting really interesting. See that pile of rocks beside the catapult? All shapes and sizes? They were just sneaking in the odd one to begin with, enough to make me wonder if I'd got all my calculations wrong.' He sighed and shook his head. 'They're smart, those Romans.'

'Sam—'

'Work to do!' He hopped off the wall and trotted down the stairs, with me tagging along behind.

'Sam! I've got to talk to you.'

'OK. Talk away.'

'Have you seen Pavel this morning?'

'Dr Pavlov?' He broke step, just for a moment. 'No.' Trotted on. 'He must be around somewhere.'

We reached the doctor's door. Sam flourished his ID, and the door swung open with a chirpy, 'Pass, friend!' Sam walked through. The door slammed shut behind him – or would have done if I hadn't stuck my foot in the way. Ouch! But I held firm.

'Who's this?' demanded the eye in the door.

'This is Luke,' said Sam. 'You must remember.'

'Must I? If you say so. What does he want?'

'A bath,' Sam lied.

'A bath? That'll be two pence, please. And could I interest you in a haircut, sir?'

'No, you couldn't.' I flashed my ID and the door swung wide enough for me to slide through. 'Haircut?' I muttered. 'What's wrong with my haircut? Who does he think he is?'

'Stay calm,' said Sam. It's just a door. It's been very simply programmed.'

I said, 'Wait a minute! You're teaching these people better ways of throwing rocks at one another, but they've got computer-operated doors?'

Sam said, 'You can always tell. All it takes is a few simple questions.' He was bending over the work bench, swept clear of glassware to make room for his paperwork, leaving the doctor with nothing to do but wander among his shelves of chemicals, muttering sadly to himself.

'Potassium chlorate!' sighed the doctor. 'And copper sulphate.' He held a jar up to the light. Shook it. Squinted at it. Shook his head, frowning. 'I'm sure I had more than that. Now, iron filings. Where did I put those iron filings?'

'Sam!' I hissed. 'Listen to me!'

'I'm listening.' His head was bent close to the table, entering figures, ruling lines, little pink tongue curling over his top lip as he joined up the points on a new graph.

I said, 'It's happening again! Like in the Colony. Stuff going missing. A jar of preserving salts – a sack of charcoal – a jar of sulphur—'

Brown eyes glanced silently up at me.

'And if you say Trust the Company; or The Company Knows Best—'

Sam, unfazed, said, 'I wasn't going to say that. I was going to say – before you interrupted – it's not just the sulphur that's missing. The doctor thinks there could be other stuff. That's why he's stock-taking. Only I don't think he kept any records of what he had to begin with.' He bent over his sums again.

'Maybe it's not just things,' I whispered. 'I can't find Pavel, either. What'll we do without Pavel?'

'Stay calm?' suggested Sam. 'This isn't easy, you know, without a computer. I suppose that's the whole point. It's not meant to be easy.'

'Sam, I'm starting to get a really bad feeling about this place.'

'Uh-huh!'

He didn't even look up.

Outside the wizard's kitchen I looked left towards the stairwell leading upwards to the sunshine. Then I looked right, down the dim, dark corridor, darker, it seemed, than yesterday, dissolving into utter blackness. And I saw a glowing patch of light, which became a flickering flame as I watched, before it bobbed away and round a corner.

So I followed it. Don't ask me why. Followed along dark, damp passageways, reminding me of our trip through the coalmine. Sounds from above fading away into silence, till there was nothing but my own breathing and a pitter-patter of footsteps up ahead. The light, diamond-bright, twinkling and dancing. Then the footsteps stopped and the light hung in the darkness. I saw it was the same little kid from the mine, with the candle in its hat, sitting cross-legged beside a heavy oak door.

'You got out, then?' I said. 'Before the flood.'

No answer.

I said, 'Well, obviously you did, or you wouldn't be here now. Mind telling me how you got here? Is there another way into this place? Or out of it?'

The kid looked straight through me.

'Go on, then,' it said, with a jerk of its head towards the door. 'Through there.'

I pushed it open. Inside, all I could see to begin with were candles guttering in the draught. Deep down in the darkness near my feet, something stirred. A voice said softly, 'Come in, then, Luke, and shut the door.' So I did. Then the voice came again, 'Don't come any closer! Get down on the floor!'

Lying on cold, stone slabs, all I could hear was a snakelike hissing. It seemed to be travelling away from me, which was good. Then came a *Bang!* – not loud, but so unexpected I almost jumped out of my skin – and a brilliant flash of light, imprinting a picture of the long, low cellar in my mind. Barrels and jars and sacks, a jumble of arrows, stone bottles and sheets of parchment, a heap of firewood, a coil of rope and one small cartwheel. Then it was candlelight and shadows again. And a smell that was vaguely familiar – smoky, acrid, sweet, all at once.

'OK, Luke. You can get up now.' I recognised the voice this time.

I called out nervously, 'Pavel?' Scrambling to my feet, 'Pavel, I've been looking for you everywhere. What are you doing down here?'

'I am conducting an experiment.' My eyes were getting

more used to the patterns of light and shade now. I could make out candlelight reflecting off his glasses; his face and hands so smeared with soot it was no wonder I couldn't make him out before, and his hair frizzed up like a birds' nest.

I said, 'What kind of an experiment?'

He ran his fingers through his birds' nest hair. 'With chemicals. All very simple.'

'Sam said the doctor thought there were some chemicals missing.'

'Sam, yes! Sam, with his trebuchet, has shown us that whatever else is odd about this place, the laws of maths and physics still hold good. Now I am trying to see if it is the same with chemistry. First we take sulphur, saltpetre and charcoal, mix them together in the right proportions, and what do we get?'

'I don't know,' I said. 'What do we get?'

'Gunpowder!' And before I could say anything more, he went on, 'But gunpowder on its own is not very interesting. No! So then we add potassium chlorate to up the temperature, and after that copper sulphate, strontium nitrate, potassium salts, to turn the flame and the smoke blue, red, violet . . .'

'Pavel—'

'After that, iron filings—'

'Pavel! Listen to me a minute! Pavel, did you send that little kid to fetch me here?'

'What little kid? I?' He paused for a moment, like he was searching his memory, just in case. Then he shook his head. 'No.'

I said, 'The guard up there was asking questions just now. Never mind the rest of the junk you stole. The bottles and the arrows and the parchment and that. Maybe he's not interested. Maybe no-one's reported it missing. It's the stuff to make gunpowder that he's interested in. He looked at me like I was supposed to know something about it.'

'Ah!' was all he said.

Was I ever going to get through to him? 'Pavel, this could be serious! They know it was you that took that stuff.'

'Interesting. They know what I am doing. And where to find me. But they don't stop me. My guess is, they are waiting to see what we will do next.'

'We've got to get out of here!'

'Careful, Luke. Even here they may be listening to us, maybe even watching.'

I gave an uneasy glance around. Pavel went on, 'Remember what you said about a rope and a diversion?'

'We *are* getting out!'

'Sh!'

'Sorry. What about Sam?'

'What about Sam?'

'What if he wants to stay?'

'You must persuade him to come with us. And, Luke!'

'Yes?'

'If anything should happen to me—'

'Nothing's going to happen to you. Is it?'

'I don't know. What I am planning here, it could change everything. If we get separated, you and Sam must stick together, no matter what. OK?'

'OK.'

'Now, off you go upstairs, and see what's going on, keep a look-out. Let's get this show on the road!'

Outside, the kid with the candle in his hat had gone again, but I managed to find my way upstairs without a guide. Took a good look around before I stepped out into the sunlight. No guards lying in wait. Nothing. Situation normal.

Pavel didn't have to spell it out for me. I'd guessed what kind of a diversion he was planning. Gunpowder and sparks and coloured lights. Fireworks! If these people really were medieval in their technology, they'd be gob-smacked. Even if they weren't, people always watch fireworks. It's human nature. Bright lights and bangers and plenty of smoke to give us cover. Everyone looking the other way. Come nightfall, we'd be out of here!

Still I couldn't help feeling edgy – more so as the day wore on and Pavel appeared with his first batch of rockets, with stone bottles to set them in. I kept an eye open while he carried them up to the watchtower. No-one seemed interested, not even the guards up on the wall, though he had to walk past them, almost. So much for his theory that they were watching to see what we did next.

Sam was still busy round the trebuchet. I wasn't going to tell him yet what Pavel was planning. You couldn't rely on Sam not to spill the beans. For the time being, this was between Pavel and me.

Pavel had fixed it so he was on evening guard duty on the landward wall. I took his grey string vest and a tin helmet that must have weighed two kilos, minimum, and stood in for him while he got everything ready. I still hadn't bought into Sam's theory that nothing could hurt us while we were here, so I marched slow, slow past the merlons, then quick, quick, quick past each embrasure – like I was dancing to an invisible band.

SIXTEEN

As a stand-in for Pavel, I guess I lacked something – about half a metre in height, for a start. But the guards at either end of the wall didn't seem too bothered. They'd been detailed to keep an eye on the enemy camp, not stuff going on inside the castle.

The sun went down and the shadows lengthened, dark enough for us to move around on the allure without anyone noticing anything odd going on. Together we opened out a wooden latticework of stars, crosses, swastikas and letters spelling out, Romans Go Home – which ought to raise a cheer from inside the castle, if it worked.

Pavel tossed me his knife and a ball of string, and told me to make the far end fast to the furthest merlon. I was just finishing – tying an extra knot for good measure – when Sam's little moon-face rose over the top of the stairwell. 'I thought it was you!' he beamed. 'Pretending you were on guard duty.'

'Not so loud,' I hissed, clapping a hand over his mouth so fast I almost sent him tumbling down again, and had to catch him by the scruff of his shirt.

'Leggo,' he squirmed. 'You're smufflicating me! What's going on?'

I suddenly had a brainwave. 'This is the big test, Sam,' I whispered. 'Pavel's worked it out. We have to find a way of escaping, using only the things we find lying around.'

'Why?'

'I don't know why. He just said, 'Trust the Company.'

'Oh!' he said. 'Right!'

At that moment Pavel touched a light to the first rocket, which soared away, fire streaming from its tail, and exploded in a cascade of coloured stars.

Everyone was caught off guard. Heads turned, eyes wide, mouths hanging open. Without giving them a chance to catch their breath, Pavel set a match to the next one. And the next. Voices started calling out to the people inside to come and see. There were gasps – 'ooh' – as each rocket shot up, exploded into coloured sparks, then died – 'aah'.

From where I stood on top of the wall, I could see the Romans edging closer for a better view. A handful of firecrackers kept them at a respectful distance. Catherine wheels spinning and showers of golden rain – more 'oohs' and 'aahs', the same the universe over.

I made fast one end of the rope and tossed the rest down into the abyss. More rockets, then clouds of smoke from Roman candles, turning from pink to green, then purple and blue. Time to go. 'Come on, Sam.'

Sam stood like he was taking root. 'Sam?' I nudged him.

'Fireworks!' breathed Sam. 'Gunpowder! Yes! Why didn't I think of it before? That would really give us an edge! Grenades fired from the trebuchet! I'd have to experiment to find the right length of fuse . . .' I didn't need to be a telepath to know which way his mind was working. History at the gallop, the nasty bits. Just give him six months and he'd have them re-fighting the great twentieth century wars.

I said again, 'Come on.'

He said, 'Come where?'

'We're getting out, remember?'

He looked at the tope, snaking down the wall into nothingness.

He said, 'I'm not climbing down there!'

I said, 'You are!'

'I can't!'

'You scared?'

'What if I am?'

Fireworks glowed and fizzed and exploded behind us, smoke thickening, eddying and billowing. Pavel was setting a light to the main display. We hadn't got much more time.

Sam risked another look down into the abyss. 'You don't even know if that rope reaches the bottom.'

'It'll reach.'

'What if it breaks?'

'It won't break.'

'What if I fall?'

'I'll catch you.'

'You go first, then,' he said cunningly.

I'd got to make him come with us. Pavel said we had to stick together and besides, if I left him here there was no knowing the damage Sam might do. In my mind's eye I could see it. Buildings crumbling. People crawling out of the ruins . . .

I heard Pavel call my name. Turned to see him launching himself towards me in slow motion.

Then the world exploded.

I remember thinking, What did I do? What did I say?

My ears went numb.

At our feet, a huge section of the wall began to crumble. Rocks floating into the air, as light as feathers. Above them a dust cloud billowing higher, blotting out the moon and stars. There was a roar like static in my ears. Then gravity took over and the rocks and bricks and stones rained down again.

I grabbed hold of Sam and peered through the dust and smoke, searching for Pavel. I called his name, 'Pavel! Pavel!' There were people all around us, scrambling over the rubble, sobbing, dragging themselves out, calling, moaning, just as I'd seen it in my mind's eye only minutes before. Little fires starting up, flickering red and yellow and orange in the gloom.

'Pavel!'

'Luke! Sam! Over here!'

Still keeping a tight hold of Sam, dragging him after me – 'See what you've done, Sam?' 'Not me! Not me!' 'See what you would have done, then?' – I tumbled over the fallen rocks towards the sound of Pavel's voice.

'Pavel? What's going on?'

'What's happening?' demanded Sam.

Pavel wiped the dust off his glasses and ran a hand through his hair. 'This way!' he said. 'This way! Let's just get you out of here.'

There were people caked in dust scurrying along, hugging close to crumbling walls, crouching low, heads tucked in, as if making themselves extra small would keep them safe. Flickering fires and columns of smoke. An unearthly howling, rising and falling, coming from all around. From high in the sky a drone of engines. Then more explosions, ahead of us, left, right and behind. We struggled on for a bit, but there seemed to be no way out. The devastation just went on and on. The smoke got thicker.

Pavel, a few steps ahead, shaking his head, muttering, 'No. I won't accept this. This is all wrong.' Suddenly he stopped, and lifting up his head he shouted, 'I don't believe this! This is not possible! This must stop! Now!' And everything did stop. There was silence all around, like the world was waiting for something terrible to happen.

'Go on, you two,' he said quietly, without turning round. 'Get out of here.'

'Not without you,' I said.

'Go on!' he said again. 'I'll be OK.'

'We can't go without you!' wailed Sam. 'We'll never find the way.'

'You'll find it. I promise.'

We stumbled a few steps, helping each other over the next crumbling bit of wall, then turned back.

The stillness went on and on. Even the dust hung in the air, waiting for the signal before it let itself go.

Pavel was smiling, looking up. 'I was right!' he said softly. 'Oh, wonderful!'

From out of the clouds above his head a small, round bomb slowly floated down. I knew it was a bomb, because of the word BOMB painted on it. And it floated rather than fell, because of the handkerchief-parachute it was tied to. Pavel was still smiling when he caught it. The last word I heard him say was, 'Yesss!'

There was a flash of light. I don't remember hearing the explosion; it was more like, for a split second, I saw the word BANG! written on the sky.

Then the noise started up again; explosions and

rumblings and people shouting and crying.

When the cloud had cleared enough for us to see, all that was left of Pavel was a pair of boots with wisps of smoke gently curling out of them. We both stood staring at them for a bit.

'He's dead, Luke,' Sam said shakily.

'No, he's not,' I said, as firmly as I knew how. 'People don't die like that! People do not explode and leave a pair of smoking boots behind. Not in real life.'

'Where is he, then?'

'I don't know!' I snapped. 'Come on. We'd better keep moving.'

'What about his boots? Should we take them with us?'

I said, 'Better leave them. In case he comes back for them, yeah?'

'Yeah.' He grabbed my hand. I didn't shake him off. 'Which way, Luke?'

Search me. Pavel said we'd know which way to go. All ways looked the same, fire, smoke, rubble . . . Then out of the murk loomed a familiar figure. Different uniform, navy blue with silver buttons. Same helmet, except for the letters ARP painted on it now.

'Come on!' said the guard. 'This way!' Off he went. We struggled along behind him till we came to a wide flight of stairs under a curving, white-tiled roof leading downwards.

'Go on,' he nodded. 'You'll be safe down there. Can't stop.' He glanced up at the sky. 'Bombers' moon!' He skedaddled.

There was a sign over the entrance. Sam read it aloud. 'Ald-wych. What do you think, Luke? Is it another misspelling?' He peered doubtfully into the gloom at the foot of the stairs. 'Old Witch, maybe?'

Aldwych. Aldwych. The name meant something to me. I'd seen pictures. I said, 'It'll be OK. Come on! We'll be safe down there. Like he said.' I plunged downwards into the half-light, leaving Sam to follow or not. Over my shoulder I said, 'Aldwych was the name of a station on the London underground railway. People used to shelter down there from the bombing in the great twentieth-century wars. But the trains kept running! Don't you see, Sam! That's our way out of here! Pavel said we'd find it. The trains kept running!'

At the foot of the steps there was a man in a peaked cap. 'Tickets, please!' he said.

I flashed my ID.

'That'll do nicely,' he said.

I said, 'the train hasn't gone yet, has it?'

'Not yet,' he said. I could hear it now, a low rumble in the distance, as I rushed on, Sam tugging at my sleeve. 'Luke! Luke, that was Dr Dee, wasn't it? What's he doing down here?'

'Search me.'

'What's going on, Luke? I don't like this. Let's go back.'

We'd reached the platform, crammed with people. People wandering about or standing still; sitting on fishing stools or deckchairs or cushions; measuring out their space for a bed for the night. There were old men clutching newspapers and old women knitting; young women carrying babies. And the crone, doling out hot soup to a line of ragged kids, who looked like they'd strayed in from *Oliver Twist*. She'd swapped the grunge for a neat, green two-piece, with matching hat, but she looked much the same. So did the soup.

The rails were humming, the rumbling getting louder. Then twin lights rushed towards us out of the pitch darkness of the tunnel, with a lighted window above and the shadowy silhouette of the driver. Dimly lit carriages snaking behind; one, two, three, four. The train clattered to a halt with something between a creak and a long drawn-out sigh. Doors slid open invitingly. No-one got on. No-one got off. The carriages were empty.

'Come on, Sam!' I tugged at his hand. 'What are we waiting for? We're out of here!'

Sam braced his feet and started pulling just as hard the other way. 'No!' He shook his head. 'No. We ought to stay here.'

'What for?'

'We should have stayed where we were. In the castle. Look what happened to Dr Pavlov!'

'What happened?'

'I don't know! That's the worst thing; I don't know!'

A voice shouted, 'Mind the doors!'

I tugged my hand free of Sam's and hurled myself aboard.

'Luke! Don't leave me!'

'Come with me, then!' I yelled back as the doors slid slowly to. I stuck my foot in the gap to stop them closing. 'Come on!'

'Mind the doors, *please*!' snapped the voice again. Still keeping my eye on Sam, in case he changed his mind, I edged my foot out of the way. The doors opened out a little, then eased shut. The train moved away, rattling and swaying, gathering speed.

We kept eye contact right up until the moment when

the train plunged into the tunnel. Into the dark. Last thing I saw was Sam's mouth opening wide, calling out: what? My name? Maybe. '*Lu-u-u-ke!' Luke! Don't leave me!*

I felt terrible. Too late! He was on his own. And so was I. Stick together, Pavel said. Here was I, letting myself be carried into the unknown. Alone.

SEVENTEEN

Carriages bumping and swaying and rattling. Darkness outside and shadows looming, forming themselves into strange shapes, like alien life-forms peering in, observing me. A feeling that, somewhere beyond all the rattling and clunking, someone was whispering about me, just out of earshot.

Stay calm, I told myself; there's nothing on Omega Seven that can harm you. Company-speak. What did they know about what we'd found the other side of the Blue Mountain? Zilch. Nada. Niente. A great, big zero.

How long had I been travelling? I don't know. Long enough to sink into a kind of doze. I jerked awake again as – we? who's we? – shuddered to a halt. The doors slid open again. I stuck my head gingerly out and took a careful look around. It wasn't pitch dark. There was a thin overspill of light from the train. And tall lamps, throwing little pools of light on to a deserted concrete platform. There were wooden slatted seats, tubs of brightly-coloured flowers, and a low building with a dusty sign over the door. I stepped off the train and edged close enough to read it. It said Waiting Room.

Behind me, the doors slid shut again and the train rattled away into the night. There was no-one to ask where this was. Or which way to the Blue Mountain; which way was home? I thought of cavemen; fingered

Pavel's knife in my pocket and felt better. I might be able to frighten them off by waving it about a bit. If I had to.

The door of the Waiting Room swung open at a touch. Inside was a bare wood floor, shiny, slime-green walls and half a dozen wooden chairs. I crept inside, jammed a chair under the doorknob so no-one else could get in and settled down to wait for morning.

When I woke up, the sun was shining through the window and I was lying safe in my own bed at home.

It felt like my own bed. Looked like my own room. All the usual clutter. Familiar noises came from downstairs. Voices, not loud enough to hear what they were saying. Then the door sliding shut behind Pa as he set off for work. I took a swift look outside to check my bearings. And saw nothing but mist, swirling right up against the window, like it was trying to claw its way in. You never get mist on Omega Seven. I blinked once and looked again and there were the familiar streets of living-units, the same view I'd expect to see, if I really was in my own little bed at home.

I decided to play along.

I got up quietly and moved to the top of the stairs. Below me I could see a figure in a powder-blue work-suit. 'Ma? She had her back to me, but the build was right. The hair was right.

I skimmed down the rest of the stairs, top speed. 'Ma?' I said.

'Sit down and eat your breakfast, Luke.' There was something about the voice. Too calm. More Sweet-as-sugar than Ma first thing.

Breakfast laid ready on the table, juice and cereal,

scrambled eggs and toast and bacon. Smelling of nothing. Tasting of nothing.

'You're not my mother,' I said. 'And this isn't home.'

The figure turned to face me and smiled a toothless smile – but quite a nice smile, considering.

'No, Luke. I'm not your mother,' said the crone. 'I am your godmother.'

'My what?' I knew my mouth had fallen open, but I couldn't quite remember how to close it.

'Your godmother. Everyone's got one; isn't that right?'

'Oh! Right!' Well, what would you have said?

'Of course that's right,' she nodded, in a satisfied kind of way, and kept on nodding. 'I'm here to grant your dearest wish.'

'My what?' I was starting to repeat myself.

She was still nodding: 'Poor boy kind to aged crone – crone turns out to be his fairy godmother—'

My *fairy* godmother? This was getting silly.

'—who offers to grant his dearest wish. That's the rule. So, name it, Luke! Whatever you want most in all the world.'

This was so weird. Like, unbe-liev-able. I said, 'This is some kind of test, right?'

A decent meal would have been pretty high on my wish list. But that would be stupid. Besides, once I was safely home I could eat all I wanted.

'If you just want to go home,' she smiled, 'you only have to say so!'

'Honest?'

'Honest!'

I could go home! Now! This minute. Just for the asking! But then, hang on a minute: what about Pavel? If

I could bring Pavel back again, unharmed . . . And there was Sam. Sam was a deek and a pain, but he was still a person. We'd been through a lot together. And the sight of his little round face and big brown eyes, his mouth calling silently after me – Lu-u-uke! – would haunt me ever after. I shouldn't have left him.

'I wish I hadn't left Sam on his own.'

I didn't even realise I was saying the words out loud. But before I could yell, 'Hang on a sec! That wasn't a real wish. I've got a better idea,' the crone had vanished. The walls were dissolving, spinning round me.

When the world settled down again, I was standing in a cold, square room. Black walls, covered in chalk marks to about head height, then travelling on up, into a deeper darkness. I couldn't see the ceiling. Sam was sitting cross-legged on the floor hunched over a chessboard. But it wasn't chess pieces he was playing with. They were dominoes. I threaded my way towards him, between patterns of matchsticks and polyominoes set out on the floor, and part-filled glasses of water, a set of scales, a Rubik's cube and the Tower of Hanoi.

'Hi, Sam,' I said.

'Oh, hi.' Like I'd never been gone.

'You OK?'

'I'm fine.' He didn't even look up. Just shuffled a couple of dominoes round the board and frowned to himself.

'Come on,' I said, 'let's get out of here.'

He shook his head. 'We can't go till I've finished this. Each time I think I've finished, there's some new problem—' He flapped a hand towards the wall. I saw the chalk marks were diagrams; equations; logic puzzles. '*A man stands on the bank of a river, with a bag of corn, a chicken and a dog . . .' 'A traveller in a country where one tribe always tells the truth and the other always lies . . .'* All the old favourites. 'Where did they all come from?' I asked.

'I don't know, do I? Will you just stop interrupting and let me concentrate!' He sighed. 'It's impossible. Look. A chessboard has got sixty-four squares, right? If a domino's the right size to cover two squares, thirty-two dominoes will cover the whole board.'

'Chessboard – dominoes. Dominoes – chessboard. Gotcha!'

He threw me a pitying look. 'Now,' he said. 'Take away the two diagonally opposite corner squares and one of the dominoes. And use the thirty-one dominoes to cover the sixty-two squares you've got left.

'That's simple.'

'I just told you it's impossible. Each domino covers one black square and one white. Take away two white corner squares and you're always going to have two separate black squares left, and one domino left over. Or vice versa.'

'Vice versa?'

'Take away the two black corner squares and you're always going to have two white ones left.'

'And a spare domino?'

'Yesss!' He suddenly picked up the board and flung it at the wall. Dominoes flew every which way. 'I'm never going to get out of here!'

'Yes, you are!' I collected up the dominoes one by one and set the board right way up again.

'Come on,' I said. 'We'll crack this thing together.

I set the dominoes out again. I shuffled them about on top of the board until the spots started doing a soft-shoe shuffle in front of my eyes, so I turned them over and started again. Each time I was left with one domino in my hand and two separate empty squares.

Sam was right. It was impossible. About stuff to do with maths, he was always going to be right.

'OK,' I said. 'You're right; it's impossible. Come on, let's go.'

'Not till I've found the answer!'

'You said there isn't one. Maybe the answer is to just give up.'

He wasn't going to let it go.

I looked at the domino in my hand: 'Hang on a minute! Cover all the squares with the dominoes, right?'

He nodded.

'That's all?'

He nodded again.

'No problem!' With a bit of help from Pavel's knife, I snapped the last domino in half and laid the two bits over the empty squares.

Sam wailed, 'You can't do that! It's cheating.'

'Who says? Cover all the squares with the dominoes, you said! Did anyone tell you you couldn't break one in half?'

'No.'

'Then it's not cheating. Game over. Come on; let's go.'

He said sulkily, 'How?' Because we really were surrounded by four solid walls. No door. No windows.

I turned back to Sam: 'How did you get in here?'

Sam shrugged: 'I don't know. One minute we were . . . and then – well, here we are, aren't we? And there's no way out, is there?'

'Shut up! I'm thinking.' There had to be a way out. I

told myself, there's always a way out! Some weak point.

Things round here did seem to have an uncanny knack of turning up, just when we needed them. If we only knew the trick of how to ask. I had a feeling Open Sesame was not going to work a second time. I tried it once out loud, just in case. I was right. Then I started thinking about that conversation I had with the crone. 'Sam,' I said. 'How does a fire feel when you've just made it up?'

'Huh?'

'Grate-full! Yeah?'

'That's terrible.'

I was suddenly so excited I felt like dancing. 'What do ghosts have for lunch?' I yelled. 'Ghoul-ash! And what do they have for dinner? Spooketti!'

'If you think you can take my mind off things by telling me stupid jokes—'

'That's not the point! The point is that you understand them! The crone didn't. When I asked her straight out, what is this place? "A castle," she said. Remember what the little kid said down the mine, when Pavel asked him what's up there? "The roof," he said. There is a way out of here! We can *make* a way out! Trust me, Sam. Do as I do. First we rub our hands together – you doing that? – till we get a little sore. Then with the saw—'

'The what?'

'The saw! You know what a saw is, don't you? Keep rubbing!' I shouted aloud, 'Are you listening to me, whoever you are? Wherever you are? We're making ourselves a little sore. A little saw! Think of a saw! Believe in it, Sam!'

And there it was, lying on the floor between us. A little saw.

Sam goggled at it. 'What now, Luke?'

'Now,' I said as I picked up the saw, 'I'm going to saw this chessboard into two halves.'

'Do you think you should?'

'I'm doing it! Straight across the middle! You're the mathematician. What do two halves make, Sam?'

'One whole?'

I nodded, still sawing away (it was only a very little saw). 'One whole. Two halves make a hole. A hole!' I yelled. 'Get it? A hole for us to crawl through. You better believe it, Sam! A hole's what you get,' I said, holding the two bits up against the wall, 'when you take two halves and put them together. What do you get?'

'A hole!' mumbled Sam as he crawled through it after me. 'This is crazy!'

'Who cares? So long as it works.'

Outside, the mist was back. We took two steps and the room – the tower – the prison, wherever we'd just been, was swallowed up. No going back. Nowhere to run. There was just the two of us, and yet . . . and yet, I couldn't rid myself of that prickly feeling between my shoulder blades that told me there was someone else.

'What do we do now, Luke?' whispered Sam. I guessed he'd got that prickly feeling, too.

What we were supposed to do was shout until we got a little hoarse, then climb on the horse and ride away. But I'd had enough of playing games. 'We do nothing,' I said. 'We don't even think. We just wait and see.'

The mist shifted and swirled, gathering itself together,

thicker in one place than the rest. The shape became a human figure, long legs striding towards us out of the mist. Pavel!

Even then I wasn't totally sure. Was this really Pavel?

'Dr Pavlov!' Sam, in no doubt, rushed towards him, arms wrapping round him, clinging on. 'You're not dead!'

'Of course not.' Pavel's smile grew broader. 'People don't explode and leave their boots behind. Do they, Luke?'

'Pavel.' I was grinning like an idiot. 'Is it really you?'

'It's me.'

'Where did you go?'

He shook his head in a bemused kind of way: 'Nowhere. Everywhere. I have been imprisoned in a nutshell, yet a king of infinite space!'

'You OK?'

'More OK than I ever felt in my life before. Just a little over-excited, that's all. Shall we go some place we can talk?'

I looked around at the featureless mist. 'Like where?' I asked.

'Anywhere you choose! I think you have worked that out by now. Just close your eyes and imagine the place where you would like to be.'

So I closed my eyes, and what floated into my mind was a picture of our old backyard, the green, green grass of home and the apple tree in the corner. I opened my eyes again and there it was, with blossom and fruit all clustering together, right down to the scar that was left from the branch that broke when I was climbing it three years ago. Flowers everywhere, like no flowers I ever saw in my life before, bright reds and pinks and purples, scrambling upwards, cascading down. And a little ruined fountain.

'My favourite place of all!' Sam squeaked.

Beyond were birch trees, mile upon mile, stretching away to infinity.

'Birch trees,' Pavel said softly, 'are what *I* miss most about home.'

I said, 'Pavel? How did you *do* that?'

He shook his head and smiled. 'Not me,' he said.

'Then who?'

'Can't you guess?'

EIGHTEEN

Pavel took off his glasses and sat polishing them carefully. 'All my life,' he said, ' – and my father, too, through his life – and my grandfather, and his father, who was part of the original SETI project—'

'SETI?' Sam interrupted.

'Search for Extra-Terrestrial Intelligence,' I said.

Pavel went on, 'Always, we have dreamed of being the first to talk with an intelligent life-form from some other planet. To understand. To share. To see the universe the way they see it.'

'Aliens?' I felt a cold shiver run down my spine.

'That depends on your point of view,' said Pavel. 'Here, we are the aliens. The intruders.'

Aliens. I knew that in all the old flat-screen movies, aliens nearly always turned out to be the answer. Aliens have kind of gone out of fashion since then. We've been disappointed too many times. But like the man said, when you've talked yourself out of every other explanation, whatever's left, however unlikely, has to be the truth.

'Omegans, then.' I looked carefully all around. 'Where are they?'

Pavel said calmly, 'They are here.'

'Here? You mean, like, here, now, watching us?'

'Now? This minute?' Sam, too, glanced uneasily about. 'Why can't we see them, then? Why don't they say something?' Like he was going to prove Pavel wrong.

Pavel said, 'Our eyes can't see them. Our ears can't hear them. But they are there.'

'A bit like ghosts?' I suggested. Not that I believe in stuff like that. Maybe I should reconsider.

Pavel nodded: 'Something like ghosts. If bats, dogs, whales, elephants can hear sounds we can't, and snakes can detect a body's heat in infrared and insects see flowers not in colour, the way we do, but in ultraviolet, why should there not be some form of intelligence living completely outside the range of what we can see and hear?'

I took another careful look around and it seemed to me that, here and there, I could just make out a slight trembling in the air. I listened hard and thought I could hear, not exactly a sound, but not quite total silence either.

'How long have they been watching us?' I wondered.

'Since the first ship from earth arrived. Think of the Blue Mountain as like a naturalist's "hide", from which he can see without being seen.'

I could imagine that pretty easily. The reason why it sometimes seemed close to, watching over your shoulder. At other times far away, beckoning.

'After a while,' said Pavel, 'they started borrowing things, to see how they worked. They always tried to put them back without anyone noticing, but sometimes they made mistakes.'

'The disappearing autocook!' Sam exclaimed.

'A football turned inside out! And my ID!'

'Rifling through the school data systems!'

'Mr Strangeways!'

'Now us.'

There was silence for a moment.

'Sam said, 'So, the Blue Mountain, is it real, or what?'

Pavel said, 'It's as real as you think it is. No more, no less. The first explorers thought it must be solid rock, because that's what mountains are made of. The harder they tried to blast a way in, the harder it became.'

I said, 'But I saw the tripedes just walking straight through, like they knew it wasn't really there!'

Pavel said thoughtfully, 'What is reality? Our brains take in light-waves and sound-waves and organise them into a picture of the world, which we call reality. But a dream, which comes only from inside your head, is also real, while you are dreaming it. A hypnotist can make you believe an onion is an apple. You bite into it, your eyes don't water, it tastes sweet. So, is it an onion or an apple? An old astronomer looks through a faulty telescope at Mars and sees canals there. And for a hundred years everyone who looked at Mars believed they could see canals. They even drew maps of them.'

I said, 'That was it! The moment you stopped believing, it stopped being real for you. Right?'

Pavel nodded, 'Right. I was no more use to the experiment.'

Sam dug me in the ribs: 'I *said* it was some kind of an experiment!'

I nudged him back 'You *said* it was the Company.'

'I was close.'

'You were a zillion miles off-beam!'

'Closer than you, anyway!'

'But why us?' I said. 'Why choose us?'

'I think we chose ourselves. Or, you two did. When you started looking at the problem of the Blue Mountain in a different way.'

'That was me,' said Sam.

'I thought of Open Sesame. I was the first one through!'

'And what did you see, Luke, on the other side of the mountain?'

I shrugged. 'Nothing much. Just some old mountain valley. I didn't know what to expect.'

Pavel nodded. 'Exactly. Then Sam arrived—'

'And the minute I saw it,' Sam rushed in, 'I started thinking of a particular place.'

'—where you had seen Romans!' Pavel cut in. 'So they showed us Romans. The same species as ourselves, but we chose not to show ourselves to them. They were too many. Too warlike. Later, they gave us a second chance. We might have made friends with the two cavemen.'

'If I hadn't thrown that stone!' I was beginning to see how it all fitted together. Using the information they'd got from watching the Colony and trawling through the school data systems, they'd built up a world for us to live in. Of course they made mistakes, like IDs and computer-operated doors.

Pavel said, 'All the time, they were running tests on us. Not pass-or-fail tests, only let's-see-what-you-do-now.'

'Like making a fire to keep warm!'

'And having to choose fight-or-flight!'

'And the castle! The castle was my idea!'

'The bath was mine,' said Sam.

Pavel chuckled. 'That gave them some problems. They searched all through the information they had for how a medieval bathroom should look. In the end, they had to settle for a Roman model.'

'Is that when you knew?' I broke in. 'Is that when you understood?'

'Not then,' he said. 'Not for sure. I think, even from the beginning, when we came through the mountain, the suspicion was there. And then, seeing Romans and cavemen and an old coalmine, then a castle, all apparently existing quite separately from one another. Just like the species on this planet. The Omegans tried to put that right by having the Romans attack the castle. Only about a thousand years out. But then there were the chemicals.'

'The only things that smelt right!' I burst out.

Pavel nodded. 'But only when I said first what I thought they were supposed to be. When I said I didn't know, there was nothing – no smell – nothing. Even then I wasn't sure. Not till the fireworks began.'

'And Sam fast-forwarded us into World War Two.'

'Both of us thinking the same thing at the same time. The Omegans must have got the idea we *wanted* it to happen!'

'But why?' I said. 'Why – any of it?'

Pavel said: 'Thousands of years ago they began another experiment. For centuries they had searched the skies, looking for a sign that they were not the only intelligent beings in the universe. At last they turned back to their own planet and made it into what they thought would be a perfect place for intelligent life-forms to evolve. A perfect climate; a few promising species; no predators; no overcrowding; no competition for food. And then they waited. For tens of thousands of years they have waited for one of these species to evolve a brain capable of more than eating and breeding.'

'And?'

'And nothing! Everything is just the same here as it was a million years ago. You know why?'

'Why?'

He chuckled to himself: 'The answer is so simple! What is it you hate most about the Colony, Luke?'

Straight off, I answered him, 'It's boring. It numbs your brain.'

Pavel beamed: 'Exactly! The Paradise Planet. No worries, no cares, no real problems. Food for the taking. No-one to eat you, lurking round the next corner. Equals, no progress. Why try and improve on Paradise? The Omegans made this place too perfect! What has made humans so smart is having problems to solve. Maybe it began when the Ice Age came and we worked out how to keep warm by wearing animal skins and making fire. Maybe it was sitting round those first camp fires that we invented language, so we could exchange ideas, ask questions about the world around us and begin working out the answers – and pass on what we knew to our children and their children. Slowly we took over the whole planet. The bits that weren't right for us to live in, we changed to suit ourselves. Give us enough time to solve the problem and we can live anywhere – at the South Pole, under the ocean, on the moon – Mars – Titan – or in deep space. We are a problem-solving species. Big problems; little problems; it doesn't matter. They all help to make us smarter.'

I thought of all that money the Company had spent on setting up the Perfect Planet for Perfect People, thinking this was going to put them ahead of the game. It was kind of funny. Aloud I said, 'So what happens now? Once we get back and tell everyone what we've found here?'

Pavel said slowly, 'I think the Company will want to keep this to themselves.'

I said, 'They can't do that!'

Sam said, 'The Company bought this planet! They can do what they want.'

I said, 'This is more important than the Company! To seek out new life and new civilisations. It's in the constitution. And now we've found one. The first ever. A civilisation that can do such mind-blowing things . . . If the Company won't go public, I'll get Pa and the telepaths on to it . . .'

'And then what?' said Pavel. 'You showed the Omegans when you threw that rock that human beings are still pretty flakey. One false move . . . You've seen the movies. So have they. Aliens are always the invaders. Bring out the military!'

'You think so?'

'They can defend themselves, can't they?' said Sam.

'And how!' said Pavel. 'Imagine an enemy that can climb inside your head, make your worst nightmares reality, bring you face to face with your worst fear, your own personal Room 101, persuade you that your dearest friend is your bitterest enemy!'

We thought about it.

'So we just tell the Company,' said Sam. 'That's best.'

'Is it?' Pavel thought carefully. 'What kind of edge would it give a Company to know how to climatise a whole planet? To trawl a person's dreams and turn them to reality?'

I said, 'You could control people their whole lives

long. They'd never have to live at all.'

Sam said, 'Yeah, well, the Omegans don't have to tell them everything. They're not stupid. You said they're millions of years ahead of us.'

Pavel said, 'There's a big difference, Sam, between wise and smart. The Company is very smart.'

Sam wasn't convinced. 'Smart enough to outwit the kind of aliens who can do all this?'

Pavel smiled quietly: 'Luke did. Only because they could not understand the difference between "saw" and "sore"; and "whole" and "hole".'

I said, 'Best if we keep stumm, right? That's what you're saying?' It broke my heart to say it. One minute, the conquering hero returns, the next the kid who overstayed his exeat.

Pavel nodded. 'I think, best if I stay here for a while and teach them a bit more about how *we* see the world.'

'What are we going to tell everyone?' I asked.

'They're bound to ask questions,' said Sam.

'Like where have we been.'

'And what happened to you?'

'Don't worry,' said Pavel. 'It's all taken care of.'

I glanced around again. There *was* a kind of shimmering in the air: there! And there, another of them. 'They're still here, aren't they?' I said. 'The Omegans.'

'They're here.'

'Wish we could see them.'

'Me too,' said Sam.

Pavel frowned: 'I don't know about "seeing them". But to see the world as they see it.' He listened for a moment. Then nodded to himself and said to us: 'Open your minds. Try and empty them completely. And maybe you will get a small taste of how it feels to *be* an Omegan.'

So I closed my eyes and tried to think of nothing. Emptiness. And slowly I began to feel a warmth inside my head. A tingling. A lightness. My feet were still touching the ground, but I was weightless; formless. I was seeing things from the outside and the inside, both at the same time. Colours I never knew existed. I forgot what shape I was, or whether I was any shape at all. If I stretched out an arm, I felt like it would go on and on, stretching on for ever, until I was nothing but an arm. Which was scary. So I tucked my arms and legs in tight and curled up into a ball so none of me could float away. And I was filled with a terrible loneliness. Alone in the universe. Just me and my kind. There were so few of us left. Then I was suddenly falling, tumbling over and over, into nothingness . . .

When I forced my eyes open again, I was sitting by the hovercar at the foot of the Blue Mountain. A short distance away, Sam was sitting too, looking like I felt.

'You OK?' I said.

He nodded, a bit dopily: 'You?'

'Dizzy. It wasn't what I expected.'

'No. The colours!'

'Colours? Yeah. And the sounds. I don't mean I could *see* the sounds. Not exactly.'

'No.'

'No.'

'That kind of floating-away feeling.'

'Yeah.'

'Yeah.'

We sat in silence for a while.

Sam said, 'It was good, though.'

I nodded: 'Let's go home.'

The hovercar had our return route already programmed in. So we climbed in, switched on, sat back and tried to enjoy the ride. As we moved out, I saw the tripedes stop what they were doing and gather round to watch us go. They looked interested – more lively than I'd ever seen them look during all the hours of video Pavel had shot. I remembered something Sam said, about the smart thing sometimes being to act dumb.

We didn't talk much. We both had too much to think about. I kept running the whole adventure through again in my mind, getting it straight so I wouldn't forget. The way the aliens always let us call the shots. Everything we said. Only once or twice did they pick up our actual thoughts. It was like what Pa said about telepathy, most of the time most people are thinking about so many things at once, they don't actually focus till they say it out loud. Was that the aliens' weak point? If you said one thing and thought another . . . Put them up against the Company suits who practise believing in three contradictory things every morning before breakfast, the Omegans wouldn't stand a chance.

Then suddenly Sam broke in, 'I can't believe the Company doesn't know what's happening on their own planet.'

I said, 'If they do know, they're keeping very quiet about it.'

'I expect they've got their reasons.'

'Yeah.'

He thought for a bit, then, 'I suppose that means we have to keep quiet, too.'

I breathed again. The aliens were safe for the moment. 'Yeah. We could be in all sorts of trouble if we don't.'

I was still trying to get some kind of story ready for the guard at the gate when we reached it. But she checked us straight through. Like it was normal for two kids to go off base and come back three or four days later. Not a mention of Pavel. She just asked us whether we'd managed to find somewhere to shelter.

'Shelter?' I said.

She nodded: 'From the rain? Perhaps it didn't rain where you were. We had quite a downpour here. Out of a clear blue sky!'

'Rain?' said Sam. 'In the day time?'

'First time ever!' she grinned. A lot of people got caught out! Nice day!'

'Nice day!' we said.

I looked at Sam and Sam looked at me.

'See you around?' I said.

Sam nodded: 'See you around.' Then he strolled off towards the dormitory block.

The rain was the big talking point of the day. It was the first thing Ma mentioned when I got home. Not that she'd been out in it, but she knew a couple of people who had.

Then Pa came in. 'Hi, Luke,' he said. 'Nice to have you back. So how did it go?'

I said, 'Er. How did what go?'

Ma said, 'The school field trip. To the Blue Mountain.

You were full of it before you went.'

'Not quite what you expected?' suggested Pa.

'Not quite,' I said.

'A bit of a let-down?'

'Not exactly.'

'So, what did you get up to?' Ma beamed.

'Oh, this and that. You know.'

Pa gave me a long, hard stare, like he did know. Telepaths aren't supposed to listen in uninvited, and like I said, most people don't know how to keep themselves down to one clear idea at a time. But sometimes they catch an image out of the ether without meaning to. Then he gave his head a little shake as if to clear it and turned away.

Ma said, 'Anyway, Ms Holloway seems pleased with what you did out there. She left a message. Wants to see you first thing tomorrow to discuss your new study programme.'

I said, 'Ms who?'

'Your new Studies Supervisor? Are you all right, Luke?'

'I'm fine. I knew we were getting a new Super. I just didn't know her name, OK? I guess she must have arrived while we were on our field trip.'

'I think she must have done,' said Ma.

I changed the subject. 'So you weren't worried about me, then?'

'Why should we be?' said Pa.

Ma smiled. 'We knew the Company were taking care of you.'

As soon as I'd grabbed something to eat (Food! Glorious food!) I hotfooted it down to the Science Complex, and flicked my ID in the general direction of the scanner.

'Oh, it's you,' said the door. 'What do you want? It's late. Nearly everyone's gone home.'

'Dr P P Pavlov, please,' I said breathlessly.

Pause.

'We have no-one of that name here.'

'Omega Ecology Survey? In the basement?'

'Er – nope!'

I wasn't going to give up that easily: 'Dr Pavel Pavlovitch Pavlov? Working for the Government of Independent Terran States? Ecologist extra-ordinaire?'

'Sor-ry! Psst! Look—' the door lowered its voice, so I had to bend closer to hear '—this is because I know you, right? And to save us both a lot of wasted time. You listening?'

'I'm listening.'

'All ecology records have been transferred to the university faculty on Osiris Three.'

'Since when?'

'You wanna get me reprogrammed? I've already said too much. Now, push off, before I call Security.'

So I pushed off home. It was getting dark anyway.

As soon as I got home, I opened up the communicator.

'Good evening, Luke!' sang out the little metal box. 'This is an unexpected pleasure! How may I help you at this unusual hour of the day-or-night (delete as necessary)?'

'Access ecology,' I said.

'Ecology. My, my! Searching . . . would you care to share with me what's brought about this sudden interest in ecology?'

'No. Just do it. Please.'

'Your wish is my command. To begin at the beginning. Ecology is the study of life-forms and their interactions with their environment. That is to say—'

I said, 'Let's cut to the chase. Give me information on university faculties. Osiris Three?'

'Osiris Three?'

'Osiris Three. On visual, please. That's it! Thank you.'

'My pleasure.'

'I can manage on my own now.'

'You sure, Luke?'

'I'm sure.'

'If you need me, just press Help!'

'I know.'

'That's good.'

I pressed Mute.

I scrolled quickly through and found what I wanted: Ecology Faculty, Osiris Three: Principal, Dr Pavel Pavlovitch Pavlov. Born Petersburg, Europe North-East, Earth. The spit-image of Pavel, only about thirty years older. No mention of a son of the same name, but then, by now, there wouldn't be. Not a trace of the Pavel I knew in all the known worlds. Until, one day, he comes strolling back from beyond the Blue Mountain, smiling that smile of his and it'll be, Pavel? Dr Pavlov – *that* Pavel! We always wondered what happened to him.

But we know already, Sam and I. Not that I have much to do with him these days. I mean, norms don't usually mix with deeks. But sometimes he catches my eye and we give one another a 'do-you-remember-when' kind of look. And I know he's thinking about the same thing I am. Hey! Maybe I am a bit of a telepath after all. Maybe everyone is, we just don't practise enough.

Anyway, just to be sure I do remember for as long as it takes till the time is right, I'm writing it all down, pencil and paper style, the way Pavel used to do. That way, no-one else can read it unless I want them to. Even if they do and they ask me if it's all true, I'll say, 'What do you think?' Maybe. Maybe I just made it up. It's like Pavel said, people need these stories.

I look out at the Blue Mountain and sometimes it seems so far away, like in a dream. I turn my back, and it's right there, peering over my shoulder. Watching and waiting.

Just in case I start disbelieving that it ever happened, I've still got Pavel's knife to remind me. The one with all the blades that he got from his grandpa. They don't make them like that any more. Not for years and years. I've asked everywhere.

Will you still remember me in a month's time?

Of course I will.

Will you still remember me in a year?

Yes.

You won't.

I will!

Knock, knock!

Who's there?

Luke.

Luke who?

See? You've forgotten me already.